*"You'll have to admit that
the night we met neither of us
was particularly cautious."*

Some emotion the prince couldn't quite identify passed over Cara's face as she nodded.

"I guess you could say that."

"About that night, I'd like to—"

"Sorry, Michael. No time to reminisce. I've got to plan these weddings and there're only a few weeks left."

"We're going to have to talk."

"I don't see why. It was a passing fling. A one-night stand. There's nothing to talk about or analyze. It was over almost before it started. Now, if you don't mind, I'd like to freshen up before my next meeting."

This time Michael took the hint.

Cara looked pale and a bit shaky and he didn't want to upset her further.

"Fine, I'll let it go for now. But you're here at the palace for these next few weeks, *cara mia*. You won't be able to run from me forever."

Dear Reader,

To me, September is the cruelest month. One minute it feels like just another glorious summer day. And then almost overnight the days become shorter and life just hits. It's no different for this month's heroes and heroines. Because they all get their own very special "September moment" when they discover a secret that will change their lives forever!

Judy Christenberry once again heads up this month with *The Texan's Tiny Dilemma* (#1782)—the next installment in her LONE STAR BRIDES miniseries. A handsome accountant must suddenly figure out how to factor love into the equation when a one-night stand results in twins. Seth Bryant gets his wake-up call when a very pregnant princess shows up on his doorstep in *Prince Baby* (#1783), which continues Susan Meier's BRYANT BABY BONANZA. Jill Limber assures us that *The Sheriff Wins a Wife* (#1784) in the continuing BLOSSOM COUNTY FAIR continuity, *but* how will this lawman react to the news that he's still married to a woman who left town eight years ago! Holly Jacobs rounds out the month with her next PERRY SQUARE: THE ROYAL INVASION! title. In *Once Upon a King* (#1785), baby seems to come before love and marriage for a future king.

And be sure to watch for more great romances next month when bestselling author Myrna Mackenzie launches our new SHAKESPEARE IN LOVE miniseries.

Happy reading,

Ann Leslie Tuttle
Associate Senior Editor

Please address questions and book requests to:
Silhouette Reader Service
U.S.: 3010 Walden Ave., P.O. Box 1325, Buffalo, NY 14269
Canadian: P.O. Box 609, Fort Erie, Ont. L2A 5X3

Once Upon a King
Holly Jacobs

SILHOUETTE *Romance*®
Published by Silhouette Books
America's Publisher of Contemporary Romance

This one's for Haley. I hope you'll always find the magic in books!
You're such an amazing young woman!

For Dr. Baxter and Carolyn Flear…there's no Philharmonic
or bowling here, but still, thanks for the inspiration!
And for Peter…hope you've enjoyed the series!

Finally, for Dort. You had the biggest heart and
such a gift for blarney. We all miss you every day.

 SILHOUETTE BOOKS

ISBN 0-373-19785-3

ONCE UPON A KING

Printed in U.S.A.

Books by Holly Jacobs

Silhouette Romance

HOLLY JACOBS

can't remember a time when she didn't read...and read a lot. Writing her own stories just seemed a natural outgrowth of that love. Reading, writing, chauffeuring kids to and from activities makes for a busy life. But it's one she wouldn't trade for any other.

Holly lives in Erie, Pennsylvania, with her husband, four children and a 180-pound Old English mastiff. In her "spare" time, Holly loves hearing from her fans. You can write to her at P.O. Box 11102, Erie, PA 16514-1102 or visit her Web site at www.HollyJacobs.com.

Dear Reader,

When I brought royalty to Perry Square and planned a trilogy, I knew I wanted Cara's story to be last. Of the three friends who make up PERRY SQUARE: THE ROYAL INVASION!, Cara's the true center of the trio. And as a tried-and-true bookworm, she's a woman after my own heart. She believes in love and has cheered on Parker and Shey in *Once Upon a Princess* and *Once Upon a Prince*. Now it's her turn to take a journey of the heart as she leaves Perry Square to travel to Eliason to plan Parker and Shey's secret double wedding. There she meets her own Prince Charming. Well, not exactly meets. You see, one night, three months ago she found, then lost, the man of her dreams. But Cara never imagined her mysterious Prince Charming was in fact a prince!

Perry Square's going on the road...going international! I hope you enjoy the trip and this final book in my Perry Square royalty trilogy!

Enjoy!

Holly

Prologue

Cara Phillips looked out the window of the plane as it made its approach to Eliason, a small European country that most of the world overlooked.

But to Cara, Eliason was magical.

A real-life kingdom.

For a minute she wondered what it would be like to know an entire land was yours...your responsibility, handed down generation after generation. To protect, to guide, to cherish.

Cara's best friend, Parker Dillon, had been born here. Parker was a princess. Princess Marie Anna Parker Mickovich Dillonetti of Eliason.

But Parker had traded away her legacy and chased after her dreams...dreams that had led her to Perry

Square in Erie, Pennsylvania, and to Jace O'Donnell, the man she was going to marry in just a month.

Four short weeks.

Their friend Shey Carlson and her fiancé, Tanner Ericson, were going to be married as well.

A double ceremony.

Cara's romantic heart gave a small twist.

Truly, Parker and Shey's romances were more than sigh-worthy.

Shey hadn't been looking for love. Especially not with a prince. Prince Eduardo Matthew Tanner Ericson of Amar had come to Erie to claim his bride— Parker. But instead he'd claimed Shey's heart.

Shey was rock hard on the outside, but that was just a veneer. On the inside she was caring, concerned and so deserved having a prince.

Cara sighed again. It was all so wonderful.

Her two best friends had found their other halves, men whom they loved and were willing to commit their lives to.

Once upon a time, Cara had thought she'd find a similar path.

For one brief moment three months ago, she thought she had.

Mike King.

He'd appeared in her life, bringing with him a whirlwind of emotion and hope…hope that she'd found what she'd been looking for. But he'd disappeared, leaving behind a longing for what-might-have-been.

She'd had just one night, one special night when

she'd believed all her fantasies could come true. On that night she'd believed in love at first sight and happily-ever-after.

Then it was morning and Mike was gone. In the light of day, Cara had awoken to the reality with a thud.

She and Mike had been just a hazy dream, a misty longing she had thought could grow into something solid. But, like a mist, the morning sun had burned her dream of him away. All she had left was a memory of the dark-haired man whose deep blue eyes had seemed to touch her soul, and the knowledge she'd deceived herself into thinking he'd felt a connection, too.

But he'd left her something tangible. Something solid and oh-so-real.

The plane touched down and Cara allowed herself one last wistful sigh.

She was going to see to it that Parker and Shey and their grooms had the most perfect fairy-tale wedding ever.

They'd have someone to love forever.

And in the end, so would Cara.

Not Mike King. He had come and gone. No, she was going to have a real someone.

She was going to have Mike's baby.

One

"Michael, stop your pacing. You look like a nervous bride on her wedding night rather than a commanding prince of the land."

Try as he might, Michael couldn't help but smile. "A bride, Marstel? You couldn't at least have said bridegroom?"

"A figure of speech," Marstel Marriott said with a smile.

Michael gave his childhood friend a lot more latitude than most employees had. As Michael's personal assistant and right-hand man, Marstel was privy to many things, but as a lifelong friend, he knew even more.

All joking aside, Marstel suddenly looked serious. "Just take a deep breath and settle down."

"Settle down?" Michael raked his fingers through his dark hair in utter frustration.

"Settle down?" he repeated. "I shouldn't be here playing host to my sister's friend. I shouldn't be playing surrogate wedding planner." His sister, Parker, was getting married soon and was sending her friend ahead to help finalize the plans. "I should be back in Erie, looking for *her*."

Her.

He didn't even know her name.

Cara mia, he'd called her.

He remembered the way she'd smiled when he'd murmured the endearment in her ear the first time.

Cara mia.

That's how he thought of her.

A chance meeting, a brief tryst…she'd altered the very fabric of his life.

"I should be out there looking for her, instead of chauffeuring around this Cara."

Just saying the woman's name grated on him, multiplying his level of frustration.

A Cara, but not his *cara mia.*

"Your soon-to-be brother-in-law has been looking for your mystery woman, but without a name…" Marstel let the rest of the sentence trail off.

He didn't need to finish it.

Michael understood that the odds were stacked against him. That night, she'd simply been *cara mia.* He'd planned to find out her real name in the light of day, but hadn't wanted to ruin the spell of that night. But in the morning she was gone. And without a name his chances of finding her were slim.

Erie, Pennsylvania, wasn't a huge city, but finding one unnamed woman in a city of one hundred thousand people was like looking for a needle in a haystack.

More than one hundred thousand people.

Michael had looked up the number online.

He was a firm believer in facing the odds, in looking obstacles square in the face…103,717 according to the last census figures.

And that didn't even take into account the outlying communities. He'd researched that as well. Millcreek, North East, Wesleyville, Harborcreek, Girard, Fairview…she could be in any one of those townships that surrounded Erie.

Somewhere among all those people was his *cara mia*.

As soon as the double wedding was over, he was going back to Erie and find her himself, even if he knew it would be like looking for that proverbial needle in the haystack.

Michael knew in his gut that, despite the odds, their one night together couldn't be the end of it. That it wasn't all they would ever have.

He'd known the minute he'd seen her that she was it for him. At that first combustible meeting, he'd been too consumed by feelings to ask the questions that had needed asking. And once he'd had rational thinking return, she was already gone.

He'd let her slip from his fingers. And because he

was on a diplomatic mission, he'd had only a few hours to search for her. A search that had proved futile.

As soon as he'd taken care of this last duty, he was going back, and he wouldn't leave Erie, Pennsylvania, until he'd found her.

Michael wasn't some hopeless romantic who fell in love at the drop of a hat. But the moment he bumped into her on the street he'd known in his gut that she was it. She was the one.

His father had found his mother in such a lightning-strike manner—found her in Erie as well, as a matter of fact. And his sister Parker had done the same when she'd fallen for the man their father had hired to find out why she wouldn't come home. Jace O'Donnell, a private detective.

Love at first sight.

He'd doubted it could happen. He hadn't been able to believe in that type of love even though he was the product of such a union. Michael was the type of man who needed more than someone else's say-so for it to be true.

So he hadn't believed…until it had happened to him.

And every day he delayed finding her was one day too many.

One more month and he'd go after her. As soon as he'd honored his obligation to his family, to his sister, Parker, he was going back to Erie and he wouldn't come home without his *cara mia*.

"They're here," Marstel announced.

The plane drew closer to the runway and touched down lightly.

Most people had to wait at luggage claim to greet the travelers. So much in the world had changed in recent years, even here in Eliason. There were new rules and restrictions designed to make air travel safer. But there were a few perks to being a prince.

Very few.

Michael and Marstel stood in the security doorway and watched as the passengers began to deplane.

Families.

Businessmen and women.

About a dozen people had come out of the doorway when he saw *her*.

He sucked in his breath, sure he was hallucinating.

"Michael, are you all right?" Marstel asked, concern in his voice.

"Her," he murmured, studying the woman. "It's her. *Cara mia.*"

"Your mystery woman?"

Three months ago, on his trip to Perry Square, Michael was supposed to have convinced his sister to come home. He could have told his father that there was no convincing Parker of anything when her mind was made up.

When he'd gotten to Erie, he'd found it wasn't just her mind that was made up, but her heart was as well. He'd seen how she'd looked when she spoke of Jace O'Donnell and he'd known that even though she might come home to visit, Parker's future was no longer in Eliason.

He'd had to leave before he'd met her friends. One friend, Shey Carlson, was marrying Tanner Ericson, the prince of neighboring Amar.

And then there was Parker's other friend, Cara Phillips.

Cara who was coming to arrange a small, private wedding ceremony for her two friends. A celebration for just family and those closest to both couples. Later there would be a more public celebration for both couples, but in one month, they'd have a secret, double ceremony.

Cara Phillips was here to help plan it.

Parker and Shey wouldn't arrive until the last minute, hoping to keep the paparazzi off the scent of what would eventually be a very big story.

It all made sense.

He'd met his mystery woman, his *cara mia*, in the park across from the shops his sister owned with her two friends. Parker's friend Cara would have been in that area frequently.

And the way his mystery woman had laughed when he'd called her *cara mia*.

Cara Phillips.

He'd known her name without knowing he'd known it. Just another indication that he was right—that this woman was his destiny.

And now she'd come to him.

What more proof did he need?

"Michael?" Marstel asked, concern still filling his voice.

"It's fine. Everything's fine now," he assured his friend.

Everything was fine.

He didn't have to find his *cara mia*.

She'd found him.

Cara got off the plane and breathed deeply. Parker used to say no place smelled quite the same as Eliason.

Maybe she was right. But at the moment, all Cara could smell was the plane's fuel. It made her stomach move a bit south of where it belonged.

She forced herself to ignore the feeling. She didn't have time to be ill. She was about to meet Parker's family—to meet royalty.

She shouldn't be nervous. After all, Parker was royal. Tanner was royal. And with their marriages, even Jace and Shey would be royal.

Through her years of friendship with Parker, Cara had learned that royalty wasn't always all it was cracked up to be. As a teen, Parker had been tabloid fodder, hounded and exploited. But through all of it, she'd had the support of her parents. Two people who put their family before their royal duties. And despite wishing their daughter was coming home to stay, they put her happiness first as well.

They'd always sounded wonderful to Cara, which was why she refused to be nervous about meeting Parker's very royal family and staying in an honest-to-goodness castle. Parker had shown her pictures, and Cara had memorized them. Not really a moat-

and-turret sort of castle. It looked more like a huge, gigantic mansion. Gray stone, ornate gardens and one small tower off the west wing.

Parker said she'd never visited all the rooms.

Cara wondered if she could manage it during her month-long visit.

Probably not. She had her work cut out for her. She was here to be a voice, to see to it the double wedding didn't become a sideshow, that it remained the small intimate ceremony her two best friends envisioned.

She was a woman on a mission. There was no time for exploring. And there was certainly no room to be nervous, she warned the butterflies in her stomach. After all, if she wanted to be nervous about something, she had bigger worries ahead of her.

She walked off the ramp and scanned the area, looking for someone who looked like they were looking for someone they didn't know. She wasn't sure who was picking her up. Parker just said someone would meet her.

She hefted her carry-on over her shoulder and started following the crowd.

"Cara mia," came a voice from behind her.

Cara stopped in her tracks and stood stone-still. She felt a jolt pulse through her body, weakening her knees. All the oxygen whooshed from her lungs.

Could someone asphyxiate from surprise?

No, this was more than surprise.

Shock.

Could she asphyxiate from shock?

She didn't want to look, couldn't stand to be disappointed, but somehow she managed to turn, to see for herself.

Mike.

Mike King in Eliason?

"You?" she said, her voice soft because, after all, it was hard to speak when you had no air in your body.

"Me," he said with a huge smile.

It almost looked as if the fink was happy to see her.

"I found you," he said.

The sense of hope disappeared in an instant as Cara remembered what Mike King had done.

The jerk.

The creep.

The love-'em-and-leave-'em cad.

Cara knew she was a quiet woman, reserved and shy. But she forgot for a second as she publicly snubbed the smiling Lothario.

"Leave me alone," she said and then turned on her heels and marched away.

She wasn't sure where she was going, but it didn't matter. She just wanted to get away from Mike King, the man who'd shown her one amazing night of passion.

Mike King, the father of her baby.

"Cara, where are you going?" he asked, obviously ignoring her command.

Maybe she hadn't been clear. She whirled around and faced him.

"Where I go is none of your concern. I want you to forget you ever met me, because believe me, I forgot you the morning I woke up alone in that hotel room."

Okay, so that was a lie.

Not just some little white lie.

A whopper of a lie.

But for the first time in her life, Cara didn't feel guilty about avoiding the truth. After all, she was crossing her fingers as she said the words, and the creep deserved to think he was so easily forgotten.

She'd never tell him that not a day went by that she didn't think of him. Not a night went by that she didn't dream of him.

"I can't forget," he said.

She kept walking.

"Go away or I'm going to call security. They'll arrest you for sure. I'm a guest of this country and I have friends in high places."

Okay, so Parker's parents weren't really friends, but she imagined they'd help protect her from a lunatic ex-lover.

"Tell me where you're going," Michael ordered, still walking by her side. His legs were much longer than hers, so she had to take about a step and a half to every one of his long, loping strides.

"None of your business," she said, trying to lengthen her own step, not wanting to be at a disadvantage. "Leave me alone, you cad."

"Cad?" he said, his smile quirking sort of sideways with amusement.

"You gigolo."

"Gigolo?" He chuckled.

That soft, throaty laughter had haunted her dreams for three months.

He placed a hand on her shoulder, as if to slow her down.

She shrugged free and tried to walk even faster. "Stop that, and stop following me."

"I can't stop following you. I was sent here to pick you up and take you to the castle, Cara Phillips."

"You work for the king?" she asked, feeling as if a lightbulb had gone off over her head. "That's why you were on Perry Square, in Erie. He sent you to try and make Parker go home, didn't he? Then you met me, figured you could have a bit of fun before you ran back to Eliason. You figured you'd never see me again. Well, let's pretend it worked, that you never met me back on the square. You can take me to the castle, then get on with your duties and forget we ever met."

"I'm afraid I can't do that, *cara mia.*"

The endearment whipped at her tenuous self-restraint. "Don't call me that," she said, hoping he couldn't sense the emotion that was riding ever closer to the surface.

"I can't do that either. You are my *cara mia,* my beloved," he said.

He reached out as if he were going to touch her again, but drew his hand back. "I've been looking for you."

"Ha."

"And I can't leave you alone because my father

asked me to assist you in whatever way suits your needs."

"Your father?" she asked. A sudden sick pitch settled in her stomach as a glimmer of an idea struck her. An unsettling, horrible, the-fates-couldn't-do-it-to-her kind of idea.

"Your father?" she repeated.

"My father, King Antonio Paul Capelli Mickovich Dillonetti of Eliason."

This time Cara didn't just feel weak-kneed, she actually sort of sagged.

Mike caught her elbow and steadied her.

An immediate awareness slammed through her system.

"What's your real name?" she asked weakly, though she knew.

"I'm Antonio Michael Paul Mickovich Dillonetti. There are a lot of titles that come after that. But my friends call me Michael."

"Well, Your Highness—"

"Michael," he corrected.

"Your friends call you Michael, and I assure you I am not your friend. I'll stick with Your Highness."

"You're right of course," he said, using what he must have thought was a soothing tone.

In reality, it was too husky, too enticing to be soothing.

"You're not a friend…." he began. "You're more."

Cara couldn't stand it.

She knew that Parker and Shey were counting on her to keep this wedding intimate and not a circus like so many other royal weddings were. But she couldn't do this.

She couldn't be here, working with him every day.

Parker and Shey would understand. They'd have to.

She turned and headed for the ticket window.

"Where are you going now?" he asked, once again on her heels.

This time she realized there was a small group of men trailing after Michael as he followed after her.

Bodyguards?

Probably. After all, a prince had to have his entourage.

A prince. The rat.

"To buy a ticket home," she said without turning around to look at him.

"You're running away again?" he asked, his voice much softer now.

She whirled around and found herself face-to-face, just inches separating them. "What do you mean *again?* I woke up and you were gone. There was nothing to do but go. I left, but I certainly didn't run away."

Had he been there, she was certain she'd have stayed as long as possible.

"I went to buy us breakfast only to return to the room and find you'd left," he said softly.

Cara felt light-headed.

"You were coming back?" she whispered.

"Of course. You were in my room, after all."

Oh, no. He hadn't left her. He hadn't used her then discarded her. Her hand fell to her stomach. Her baby's father wasn't a scum-sucking Casanova.

Another thought occurred to her.

Her baby's father was a prince.

Even worse, he was the heir to the Eliason throne.

Cara groaned as she realized that her baby was, in fact, royalty as well.

Oh, no, what had she done?

The blood rushed from her head and Cara did something she'd never done before. She fainted.

Two

There wasn't much in life that scared Michael.

All right, he wasn't overly fond of heights. But although he always avoided the window seats in planes, he dealt with the fear and never let on that he was bothered.

But at this moment, he didn't know how to hide his fear, much less deal with it. Cara collapsed in his arms and it was a thousand times worse than any height he'd ever experienced.

He eased her down on the ground without releasing his hold on her.

"Call an ambulance," he barked.

Marstel was on his mobile before he even finished the sentence.

Satisfied help was on the way, he focused all his attention on Cara. Her eyes fluttered and then opened.

He inhaled deeply and finally felt as if he could breathe again.

"Cara," he whispered.

"What happened?" she said, trying to sit up.

"Stay still. You collapsed. Marstel is calling for an ambulance."

"No. I don't need an ambulance, I'm fine. It was just a long flight. I'm sure that's all."

"If your collapse was due to just a long flight, I suspect more of the people on the plane would have collapsed. But as far as I can tell, yours is the only body on the floor. You need to see a doctor."

"I don't," she said, sitting up, even though he tried to keep her down. "Let go."

"Cara, you're seeing the doctor."

She struggled to her feet, looked a bit unsteady for a moment, then stood firm and glared at him. "I won't."

Michael stood as well and faced her.

This Cara, spitting mad and glaring at him, didn't quite match the mental image of the sweet woman who'd spent one passionate night in his arms. It was clear Michael had things to learn about Cara.

"You will see the doctor," he said just as firmly. It was a tone he rarely used, but it had always produced the desired result, in the past.

Obviously, not this time.

Cara crossed her arms over her chest and said, "Listen, Your Highness, just because you're a prince, doesn't mean I'm going to play the loyal subject. I'm not seeing a doctor."

She glanced past him and noticed Marstel, phone still in hand. "Call off the ambulance, I won't get in it. They'd be wasting a trip, and it could endanger someone who really needs help."

Marstel looked from Cara to Michael, who just shrugged. "Fine, call it off. I'll have Dr. Stevens meet us at home."

Cara shot him a small, brittle smile. "I hope you're having him meet you for tea, because he's not touching me."

She whirled around and started down the hall toward baggage claim.

"Are you always so stubborn and argumentative?" Michael asked, easily matching her pace.

Her expression softened. "Believe it or not, no. I'm generally quiet and easygoing."

"So, it's only me who is blessed with seeing this side of you?" He shot her a grin.

She shrugged. "Guess so."

She wore a small smile, though he could see her struggle against it.

It wasn't much of a smile, just a brief upturn of her lips, but it was a start. A quick reminder of the woman he'd known.

"Lucky me," he said in a teasing voice.

"Why are you following me?"

"I'm your ride home, remember?" he said. "You have decided to come home, right? I mean, you don't want to let your friends down, do you?"

The smile was gone now along with his gentle *cara mia*. The real Cara Phillips was back and said, "I am going to the castle, but only because I love Parker and Shey. But I'm not going with you. I'll take a taxi."

"There you go, being argumentative again."

"I wouldn't have to be argumentative if you weren't annoying."

"And I wouldn't seem nearly so annoying if you weren't so stubborn and argumentative."

"I guess we have a stalemate," Cara said.

"So, why don't you simply get in my car and let me take you home?"

"If I do, will you leave me alone once we get there?"

"I can't promise that, but I will promise to give you some time to settle in before I start annoying you again."

She sighed. "Fine."

"Then come with me. Marstel will arrange to have your luggage delivered."

"Whatever."

Looking more like a woman on her way to the gallows than a woman who'd just found out she was being pursued by a prince, Cara came along quietly, but the petite brunette's flashing green eyes seemed to radiate all the words she was holding back. They were seething just beneath the surface, ready to explode at any moment.

He smiled and admitted to himself, he liked that she wasn't intimidated by him.

Too many of the women he'd dated had either been awed by his position, or had sought him out hoping to capitalize on it. That one night with Cara he'd known that she'd seen him…just Michael, not the prince. She didn't look overly awed by the fact he was royal. And she certainly didn't seem intent on capitalizing on it.

As-a-matter-of-fact, she was put out by it.

"Come with me, sweetheart," he said, taking her arm, feeling as if everything in his life were suddenly on track.

She jerked her arm away, sent him a scathing look, then followed him as he made his way toward the car.

Michael wasn't sure if round one of their first fight was a win, a loss or a draw, but he was looking forward to seeing what happened in round two.

Cara glanced at the man standing next to her in the hallway of the castle. Parker's home was as grand and wonderful as she'd pictured it. Unfortunately, some of her pleasure at arriving was diminished given the company she was keeping.

To think, she'd had fantasies for the last three months about finding her Mike. Fantasies where she'd run into him on Perry Square. Just bump into him. He'd look at her and whisper, *cara mia* and pull her into his arms. He'd profess his undying love and apologize for leaving her that morning. She of course would forgive him and when she told him about the baby he'd cry with happiness. A manly sort of crying. Really only a tear or two in his eyes as he professed to love her and their child forever.

She'd never have that particular fantasy again.

Now all she wanted to do was get some distance from Mike…Michael. The prince. Maybe once she got out of his vicinity she'd be able to think again.

She scanned the grand entryway. Her whole apartment would fit in it. Parker's and Shey's as well.

She'd been so excited to be visiting a castle, staying in one. And the impressive gray structure had barely blipped on the radar of her thoughts. All she could do was wonder what on earth she was going to do.

Her fantasy lover hadn't deserted her. He claimed he'd been looking for her.

Her Prince Charming *was* a prince.

And she was carrying his child.

She had to tell him. She knew that much. But not quite yet.

Soon.

As soon as she figured out just what she was going to do.

Maybe she'd better wait until she was back in the States to tell him. Maybe he'd want to keep the baby. After all, the child growing in her womb was his heir.

What were the laws regarding parental rights in Eliason? And did a prince have to follow them?

She didn't know.

Cara had thought being a single mother was as complicated as her life could get.

She was wrong.

"Cara Phillips, may I present my mother, Her Royal Majesty—"

"Cut it out, Michael," his mother said sternly.

Michael and Parker's mother didn't look queenly at the moment. As a matter of fact, she was wearing a battered pair of jeans and a Mercyhurst sweatshirt.

"Cara, dear, I've heard so much about you. Call me Anna." She enveloped Cara in a hug. "I've so longed to meet you. You've been such a good friend to my Parker."

"Your Majesty—"

The queen cleared her throat.

"Anna," Cara corrected herself with a sheepish smile. "I'm the lucky one. Parker's the best."

"Is she truly happy with her private investigator?" the queen asked with a motherly concern.

"Yes, I believe she is. When Parker and Jace look at each other, you can see…" She stopped. She wasn't sure how to put it without seeming like a hopeless romantic.

"You can see the love?" the queen asked.

"Yes." Cara couldn't resist a small sigh.

"That's all I ever wanted for her. That she'd find a place to belong and someone to belong with." The queen looked toward a dark-haired man in crisply creased Dockers and a dark blue polo shirt striding toward her. "There's nothing more important."

"Is this her?" the man asked.

"Yes. Paul, this is Parker's friend, Cara. She'll be working with Michael and me on the wedding details."

Paul.

The king.

Darn. Cara wished she'd asked Parker the proper protocol. Should she bow, curtsy?

She was saved trying to figure it out when the man thrust his hand in her direction. "Cara, we've heard so much about you from our wayward, stubborn daughter."

Cara shook his hand and smiled. "And I've heard a lot about you."

He chuckled. "I imagine you have."

From what she'd heard from Parker over the years, she knew any stubbornness Parker possessed was genetic, inherited from her father.

"Now, Cara, let's get you settled and then I'll show you what I've already accomplished," the queen said. "Michael's been my errand boy, and we've really made some progress. We'll—"

"I think," Michael said, interrupting his mother, "that it would be better for Cara to take a rest rather than jumping into work. She passed out at the airport."

"What?" the queen and king said in unison.

"I've sent for the doctor," Michael assured them.

Cara caught the look of triumph he shot her. The ha-ha-I-won-this-battle sort of look.

"It was simply a long flight," she said. "I don't need a doctor. I don't need to rest. I just want to get down to the details."

The queen shook her head. "Oh, no. Not until you've been checked out. What would Parker say if she arrived and found you ill?"

"I—"

"Don't argue," the king instructed. "My daughter would blame me if something happened to you, and I can get in more than enough trouble with her without your assistance. So, you'll see the doctor and get his clearance before you lift a finger or look at one wedding plan."

"Really, I'm fine," Cara protested, though no one seemed to notice.

"Dr. Stevens will be the judge of that. Now, come with me, dear. We'll get you settled," the queen said, putting an arm over her shoulder and leading her down the hall.

Michael, the big tattletale, smirked at her as they walked past him, as if he'd gotten one over on her.

Cara had the overwhelming urge to stick her tongue out, but she resisted. She was a grown-up, after all.

She'd see their doctor. He'd give her a clean bill of health, of course, then she'd get on with planning the wedding of the century, then go home to Perry Square.

Parker's mother led her through a maze of halls and up a set of stairs.

"I may need a map," Cara murmured.

The queen laughed. "I felt the same way when Paul first brought me here, but you'll get the hang of it soon enough."

She stopped in front of a door. "This will be your room." She opened the door with a flourish.

"Oh, my." Cara tried to take it all in.

It was the room every little girl dreamed of. A room fit for a princess.

A canopy bed, a huge bay window, complete with window seat…and a wall full of bookshelves. For a lifelong bookworm who owned a bookstore, it was the perfect room.

She just stood in the doorway and took it all in.

"Parker suggested you might enjoy this room the most," the queen said.

"It's lovely."

"Your luggage has already been sent up." She gestured to Cara's suitcases that were sitting next to the bed. "I can help you unpack, or send someone to help you if you prefer."

"No, really, I'm fine, no matter what Michael says." Some of her pleasure over the room faded as she remembered the total mess she'd gotten herself into.

"If you're fine it won't hurt to let the doctor take a look, will it?" the queen asked gently. "It will ease my mind."

Cara admitted defeat. She could fight Michael, but not his mother.

"I'll see him," she said. "But only if we can get to work after he laughs at all your worries and assures you I'm fine."

"You've got a deal," the queen said with a smile. "I'm so glad you're here. I've missed my daughter and hope you'll fill me in on her life and about this man she's so taken with."

"I'll tell you what I can," Cara promised. "You're

going to love Jace, I promise. When you see them together, it's so obvious that they're right for each
other. It sort of shimmers there for anyone to see.
She's happier than I've ever seen her."

The queen smiled. "Her happiness is all I ever
wanted. Now, go rest and I'll send the doctor up as
soon as he arrives." She left and closed the door
softly.

Cara took in the room.

It was beautiful. She walked up to the shelves and
admired the books. Leather-bound volumes that
begged to be held and admired for the sheer beauty
of their construction, as well as their content.

Normally Cara wouldn't be able to wait to get her
hands on them. But right now she had too much on
her mind to enjoy them. She sat down gingerly on
the bed. It was warm and inviting. Too inviting to resist. She lay back and closed her eyes.

How on earth had she gotten here? The small-
town daughter of two academics was now in a castle, surrounded by luxury.

A castle that was the family home of her own
child's father.

A loud knock on her door awoke Cara with a start.

She had a momentary attack of *where-the-heck-
am-I?* before she remembered she was in Eliason to
plan Shey's and Parker's weddings.

And that she had found Michael, or rather, he had
found her.

Someone knocked on her door again.

She sat up, smoothed her hair as best she could and said, "Come in."

A man with beachboy-blond hair that looked as if it could use a cut, bright blue eyes and a ready smile rolled a very sporty wheelchair into the room.

"Cara Phillips?" he asked.

"Yes."

"I'm Dr. Stevens. Tommy Stevens." He wheeled right up to her bed and extended his hand.

Cara took it and shook. He had a firm grip.

"Nice to meet you," she said. "And I'll apologize up front for the inconvenience. I'm absolutely fine, Doctor."

"Call me Tommy. And I'm sure you're right, but why don't you let me do a brief check just to put your hosts' collective minds at rest. Additionally, you're doing me a favor. I love having a reason to make a house call to the castle. They always offer me something to eat on my way out, and if you've ever eaten hospital food, you'd know what a perk having access to the royal kitchen is. Marta, the cook, has a crush on me, and spoils me with treats."

Despite her annoyance at being forced to see a doctor, Cara couldn't help but laugh. "So, basically you work for food?"

He grinned. "Exactly. And you wouldn't want to deprive me, would you?"

"No," she assured him. "You don't work exclusively for the family?"

"No. They're a very healthy bunch. I have a private practice. I make house calls because it's easier than having their security clear my office for a visit. So, now that I've charmed you with my winsome bedside manner, do you think I could convince you to have a seat over here, please."

Giving in to the inevitable, Cara sat in the chair next to the bed, which placed her eye to eye with the doctor.

Not sure how intensive his exam would be, Cara had a sudden worry and asked, "Before we start, I need to know that patient-physician privilege works the same here as it does in the States? I mean, you can't go divulging my health concerns without my permission, right?"

Tommy smiled reassuringly. "Yes, we do have the same rules here. I won't say a word about you or your health without your permission. So, I take it that you have a condition I should know about?"

"Yes," she said, hesitating, not sure how to say it. She hadn't told anyone yet, not even Parker and Shey. She wanted them both to enjoy their weddings without worrying about her. And she knew they'd worry a lot.

"Well, you see, I'm pretty sure I know why I fainted, and it really isn't anything to worry about. I've had periods of light-headedness the past few months, and I think this one was worse simply because of the length of the flight."

He waited, not pushing or prodding, just waited for her to finish.

Cara had always trusted her gut feelings. She'd trusted them when she'd met Parker and Shey. She'd trusted them when they'd decided to open Titles and Monarch's, their bookstore and coffeehouse respectively, after graduation. She'd trusted her feelings the night she'd met Michael.

And she realized she liked this doctor and once again relied on her gut feeling. "I'm pregnant."

Tommy Stevens didn't even blink an eye with surprise. "About how far along?"

"Three months. I saw my physician before I left Erie and she said there was no reason I couldn't make the trip. She put me on a prenatal vitamin and I promised to see her again as soon as I get home next month."

"Well, that could explain things, but I'd rather take your pulse, blood pressure and such, if you don't mind."

"I don't," Cara said, realizing that having some assurance that everything was all right would be a relief. "Whatever you think is best. But I'd prefer that no one knows about the pregnancy. I haven't even told the father yet. And I didn't want to take anything away from the wedding."

"Mum's the word," he said, actually making the motion of twisting a key over his lips, then tossing it over his shoulder.

Cara laughed. "Thanks so much."

As the doctor opened his bag and took out a stethoscope, he said, "Did you ever hear the one about the doctor and the porcupine…"

Michael stood outside Cara's room his hand poised to knock, when a loud peel of laughter rang out. There was a murmur of voices, then more laughter.

He knew his mother wasn't in the room with Cara. He'd just talked to her and she'd said the doctor had arrived.

Cara was laughing with the doctor.

Michael didn't like it.

The doctor was supposed to be checking her over, not doing a stand-up routine.

Michael had imagined finding her. The slow smile he'd witnessed their one night together would again light her face and she'd welcome him with open arms. Instead, the woman laughing so easily next door with the doctor had been distant and wary when he'd found her at the airport.

Dating women had never proven to be much of a problem. Finding the right woman had been next to impossible.

Other than a short stint at a university in the States, where he'd got a taste for what Parker had had, Michael spent his adult life dating as a prince. His title was the first thing women knew about him. He frequently felt like more of a trophy than a person. Something they could show off to their friends. But Cara had only seen him as Mike, and he knew in his heart of hearts she'd felt something that night, just as he had.

Cara had wanted just plain old Mike King. Not Michael Dillonetti, future king of Eliason.

He'd never before felt anything like his reaction to her. There had been an instant connection. He wanted a chance to allow it to grow. He wanted to get to know more about her, and to share himself with her. He wanted Cara to continue seeing him, not the prince.

Parker had chosen a different way of life than what she'd been born to. As the heir to the throne, Michael didn't have that luxury. As much as he had grand plans for his country—increasing tourism and technology being two of his highest priorities—he had much smaller personal goals. Someone to love, who would love him in return—him, not his title nor his wealth. A relationship like the one his parents had. A family.

They seemed like small goals—ones most people had. But for him they had seemed out of reach until he met Cara Phillips.

The low murmurs in the room were punctuated by another burst of laughter.

He knocked on the door.

"Come in," Cara called out.

Michael walked into the room and was unprepared for the emotion that poleaxed him as he spotted Dr. Stevens and Cara sitting together.

Cara's smile died immediately when she saw who had entered.

"What do you want?" she asked, no smile or sign of greeting.

"I just came up to check on you."

Her eyes darted toward the doctor then back to him. "I'm fine."

"Dr. Stevens?" he asked, not quite believing her.

The doctor shot Cara a strange look, then turned

to Michael. "She's absolutely fine, but I'm running a few tests just to be sure."

"What kind of tests?"

Cara thrust out her arm and he noticed the smiley-face bandage in the crook of her arm. "He drew some blood and is going to test for anemia. That could explain my light-headedness."

There was something the two of them weren't telling him. Michael could sense it.

"What else?"

"Nothing else," Cara said. "Now that you've satisfied your curiosity, if you don't mind…"

She left the sentence hanging, an obvious invitation to leave her room.

"I don't mind at all," he said, taking a seat in the armchair. "Thank you for coming over so soon, Dr. Stevens."

The doctor took the hint and packed his bag. Before he left, he took a card from his pocket and handed it to Cara. "If you need anything, have any problems at all, call me. The top number is my office, the bottom number is a private line. Call anytime of day or night."

"Thank you, Tommy."

"It was my pleasure," he assured her, then gave Michael a quick nod and left the room.

"*It was my pleasure,*" Michael mocked.

"You're the one that forced me to see him," she said. "I enjoyed meeting Tommy."

"That's another thing. Tommy. Not even Tom. I've known the man for at least five years and have always called him Dr. Stevens. You've known him half an hour and he's *Tommy*. What was going on between the two of you?"

"I was assured that doctor-patient privilege is the same here in Eliason as it in the U.S., so I guess that makes what was going on between the two of us my business, doesn't it?"

"I'm concerned, Cara." Michael knew that was an understatement. Concerned didn't even begin to define the heart-stopping fear he'd felt when she'd fainted. And though she seemed fine, the fear hadn't abated much.

Her look softened a little and for a moment he thought she was going to be reasonable. Instead, she said, "Don't be concerned. You heard the doctor, I'm fine."

"I don't think he'd be doing more tests if he was one hundred percent sure of your fineness."

"He's just being cautious. I think it must be a trait of your country."

"And you say you've met my sister, Parker?" he teased. "If caution is a national trait, it's one that totally passed her by."

Cara laughed, much to Michael's delight.

"Maybe it's a trait that's connected to the Y chromosome?" she asked.

"Maybe. But you'll have to admit that the night we met neither of us was particularly cautious."

Some emotion he couldn't quite identify passed over her face as she slowly nodded.

"I guess you could say that."

"About that night, I'd like to—"

She sprang from the chair. "Sorry, Michael. No time to reminisce. I've got a clean bill of health and need to find your mother and talk about the wedding. Two ceremonies in one and only a month to plan them. I've got lots and lots of work to do."

"We're going to have to talk about that night."

"I don't see why. It was just a night. A passing fling. A one-night stand. There's nothing to talk about or analyze. It was over almost before it started. Now, if you don't mind, I'd like to freshen up before the meeting with your mother."

This time Michael took the hint and stood.

Cara looked pale and a bit shaky and he didn't want to upset her more than he suspected she already was.

"Fine, I'll let it go for now. But you're here for a whole month, *cara mia*. You won't be able to run from that night forever."

"I'm not running. I'm simply stating the truth. I'd prefer keeping my visit to your country on a completely professional level, if you don't mind."

"Ah, *cara mia*, I do indeed mind." He took her hand and before she could pull it away, he planted a light kiss on it. "I'll see you tonight at dinner."

He left her standing in the middle of the room looking a bit shell-shocked, and still far too pale for his peace of mind.

He knew there was more to the tests Dr. Stevens—Tommy—was running. He hurried to try and catch the good doctor before he left.

Michael wanted answers and he wanted them now.

Three

Cara had planned to avoid Michael, at least until she figured out what to do. But avoiding the determined prince wasn't easy.

Three days after her leave-me-alone request, she had to admit a momentary defeat, but she didn't accept it gracefully. She glared at him as he sat across from her in the limo, his assistant next to him.

Michael's mother was by her side, talking excitedly about the double wedding, oblivious to any tensions in the car.

"…Morgan has been designing my clothes for years. I think you'll like her plans for Shey's gown and Parker's. And of course, as bridesmaid, she's got something very special in mind for you."

"I can't wait to see it." Cara tried to sound enthusiastic for the queen's sake, but wasn't sure she quite pulled it off.

It was all Michael's fault. He was staring at her with an intensity that made even a normal conversation difficult.

"Thanks so much for letting me tag along," Michael said. "It made sense to carpool. And I won't need the car long. When would you two ladies like to be picked up?"

"About two hours should allow us enough time to look over all Morgan's sketches, and permit her to take Cara's measurements."

Cara knew it was ridiculous, but she found herself blushing anyway as Michael grinned and raised an eyebrow at the mention of her measurements.

His assistant, whether by chance or design, changed the subject from Cara's fittings to guards.

"They've already cleared the building?" he asked the queen.

"Yes. There are two guards already there, and another two in the car behind us."

"The king asked that I request you don't try to elude them today." Marstel glanced nervously in the queen's direction, as if he were afraid of her response.

"I promise," she told the dark-haired man. She turned to Cara and explained, "When I first arrived in Eliason, I found having bodyguards extremely difficult to deal with. On occasion, I would lose them. Even after all these years, my husband still feels the need to remind me to behave."

"All these years?" Michael asked. "I believe just last month you lost your guards and—"

"Spent the afternoon at the children's shelter. Bodyguards make the children nervous. They're intimidating."

"But they're a way of life," Michael maintained. "Just another part of our position."

"Do you like being followed?" Cara asked Michael, even though she'd told herself she was going to totally ignore him.

"No, I can't say I enjoy being watched so closely, but it's just another facet of my life. And Marstel, in addition to being my assistant, also doubles as security, and he's not overly intimidating."

"Hey," Marstel protested with a laugh.

"You intimidate me," Cara assured him sweetly.

He grinned. "Thanks."

She turned her attention back to Michael. "Parker hated this kind of thing."

He nodded. "Yes, she did. And I'm truly glad she's found a life, found someone who makes her happy."

"What about you?" Cara asked. "Does this life make you happy?"

The question sort of slipped out, but she wasn't sorry she'd asked. She wanted to know. Was this life—a life her child might someday become a part of—one that a person could find happiness in?

"There are facets that provide me with a sense of accomplishment and a great deal of gratification. There are others that are hard to bear, the restriction on my freedom is one of them." He paused and seemed to weigh her question. "On the whole, yes, I'm happy. Could I be happier?" He looked directly at her. "Yes."

Cara's breath caught for a moment with the intensity of Michael's gaze. When he finally blinked, she felt herself pulled back into focus and pressed. "But if you had a choice, would you choose this life?"

"Unlike Parker, I don't have a choice. This is the life I was born into. I have a duty to my country, one I wouldn't set aside even if I could."

"Duty," Cara echoed.

"My son always does his duty," the queen assured Cara. "No matter how he feels about it."

Cara wondered what Michael would feel his duty to the baby was—what his duty to her would be. She wasn't sure, but she was positive she'd never want to be seen as anyone's duty.

That night, dinner was a quiet, family affair. The king, the queen, Michael and an older gentleman Cara had yet to meet.

"Cara, dear," the queen said as she entered the dining room. "I'd like to introduce you to one of our dearest friends, Ambassador Bartholemew McClinnon."

The ambassador stood and held the chair next to him out for her. "Actually, I *was* the ambassador. Now, I'm just an occasional visitor who's looking for a free bed, and some fishing."

She could hear a touch of a southern accent in his voice. "You're from the States?"

"Born and bred. I understand you're one of Parker's friends. A partner in Monarch's and Titles?" He chuckled. "I love the names."

"My sister always was a bit warped," Michael said.

Cara didn't leap to Parker's defense. She didn't even look in Michael's direction. Maybe if she tried hard enough, she could forget he was across the table from her.

But as the dinner went on, it became apparent that Michael was indeed unforgettable. His presence was palpable, even as she conversed with the ambassador.

She learned that the ambassador had come to Eliason years ago. She also learned a lot about fishing. It might have been more than she needed to know, but listening to the men's fish stories, she couldn't seem to mind.

"…And then there was this time I went shark fishing," Michael said. "You should have seen the one I caught. I swear, it made Jaws look like a guppy."

Cara couldn't remain aloof, as much as she might want to. She laughed right along with everyone else.

Michael wore a mock-insulted look, but continued on. "Really. The beast was huge. Practically capsized the boat as I tried to reel it in."

"You know," said the ambassador, "I've heard my share of fish stories—mainly from your father—"

"I do not exaggerate my skills," the king assured them all. "I don't need to. Having fished with both of you, I assure you, I don't worry about who is the most accomplished fisherman. There's no contest."

As the three men quibbled over their fishing abilities, Cara couldn't help but study Michael. Something warm coursed through her body.

Watching him joke with his family, listening to his laughter. The feeling spread.

It wasn't the hot spear of desire she'd felt when she'd first met him.

It was something else. Something more.

A feeling she wasn't prepared to explore.

A feeling she was going to do her best to put aside.

"So how are you getting along with my brother?" Parker asked a week and a half after Cara had arrived in Eliason. "He's the best, isn't he?"

Cara held the phone to her ear, silent for a moment as she tried to think of a diplomatic answer.

"Uh, he seems nice enough," she finally said. "I mean, I've barely spent any time with him. Like I said, your mother and I jumped right into the wedding plans. She's great," she added, no hedging this time.

Cara already loved Parker's mom. The queen, a former Erie resident, had a warm, easygoing nature.

Cara would have loved nothing more than to ask the older woman for advice, but she couldn't. Parker's mom would be her baby's grandmother.

And Parker would be the baby's aunt.

And Cara still hadn't told a soul other than Tommy.

Things were far too complicated. But after ten

days, she was no closer to figuring out what she should do.

Cara wanted to tell her friend so much, but she knew when the announcement was made attention would shift to her, especially now that she knew Michael was the baby's father.

She wouldn't take anything away from Shey's and Parker's weddings, so she wouldn't say anything for a while yet. There was still time.

"Cara, honey, are you there?" Parker asked.

"Yeah. Sorry. I'm just tired. Must be jet lag. You'd think that ten days here would have acclimated me though."

A week and a half. Ten days of making plans and trying to avoid Michael.

Unfortunately, Michael seemed bound and determined to be as unavoidable as possible. He attended every family meal. Even his mother commented on what a rarity that was. She used his parents and whatever guests they had as buffers. The ambassador had become a special favorite.

But it wasn't just meals. Michael carpooled with them into St. Mark's as often as possible. He dropped into his mother's office to *help* with the wedding plans.

It seemed wherever Cara was, Michael wasn't far behind.

The queen had been right when she said Cara would learn to navigate the castle soon. Actually, Cara had memorized the layout within days, asking servants about shortcuts and little-known routes.

Taking small back corridors in order to try to avoid Michael, aka her personal stalker-wannabe, had become a part of her daily routine.

"Or this tiredness," Parker said, "could be related to the whole fainting thing in the airport."

"How did you—" she started to ask, then cut herself off. "Michael."

She shouldn't be surprised. He'd tattled to his parents the day she arrived, so it made sense that he'd call Parker and rat her out with his sister as well.

Or maybe she should be surprised that it had taken him a week and a half to tell Parker.

She'd have thought he'd have done it sooner. He seemed convinced there was some big secret Cara was keeping from him. She'd like to be annoyed, outraged even, but the fact that he was right made it tough.

"Your brother exaggerates. It was just jet lag," Cara reassured Parker.

"Honey, I've flown all over the world and never fainted because of jet lag. I talked to Shey and we both had noted that you seemed a bit tired before you left. What's wrong?"

"Nothing," Cara said, more guilt hitting her like a brick. She'd never kept secrets from her friends. But this once she didn't have a choice. She had to figure things out in her own mind before other people found out.

"You're imagining things," she continued. "I swear I haven't fainted again. That first day at the airport was just a fluke. I'm fine."

"I don't think so," Parker said softly. "I mean, if

it was just me, maybe. But Shey noticed as well. We both feel guilty that we were so wrapped up with Jace and Tanner we didn't push you for answers when you were here."

"Nothing's wrong. I made it to Eliason just fine. I'm having the time of my life. I love your parents. The wedding plans are coming right along. That's your update. Everything's just fine."

"I wish you'd talk to me," Parker said wistfully. "We're worried about you."

"I'm a big girl, Parker. I can handle myself."

Sometimes her friends forgot that. Cara knew she was quiet, she didn't like a fuss. Parker and Shey had always taken her under their wings.

This time she had to fly solo. She had to figure out what to do on her own.

"If you want to talk, I'm a phone call away," Parker reminded.

"I know. How's the store?" she asked, hoping to change the subject.

While she was gone, Parker was taking over the duties at Titles. Shey had Monarch's covered. They were both training new help so that both stores would be attended to while they were all in Eliason for the wedding.

"I hope I don't mess things up here—I usually work more in the coffee shop."

"You're doing fine," Cara assured her. "But don't forget, I have that big shipment in on Thursdays. Remember to check the dates. Some of the books can't be shelved until—"

"Until specific dates. I know. The store's fine." She paused a moment and added, "I wish I was sure you were."

"I am absolutely perfect. I'm having a blast planning a wedding for my two best friends. But now I'm going to bed. I'll talk to you in a day or two."

"Okay," Parker said, not sounding convinced at all about the perfectness of Cara's life. "Bye."

"Bye."

Cara hung up and sat, staring at nothing in particular. Her mind chased itself round and round, trying to decide what to do.

Her hand slipped to her stomach. It felt a bit rounder today she thought. She stopped. What was that?

It was just the slightest flutter.

The baby?

There it was again.

Emotions welled up in her chest. Love. Longing. Excitement. Terror.

They bubbled over each other, mixing up and overflowing. Cara didn't know what to do with the jumbled mess and finally gave in to the tears that were filling her eyes. She started to cry.

Her baby. It was moving inside her, almost as if it knew she needed comfort and wanted to remind her that no matter what was going on, she had someone who belonged to her, someone she could love with no hesitation.

Her baby.

She lay down and waited until it moved again. It

was amazing. A miracle. She wished she could tell someone.

Not just someone.

Michael.

She wanted to run to him and tell him their baby had moved.

This little person they had made on that one night of passion they'd shared.

Cara had never done anything like what she'd done with Michael.

A one-night stand.

It was foolish. Out of character. Utterly stupid. But she couldn't regret that their one night together had produced something so special.

"I don't know what's going to happen, but I swear, I'll do what's best for you. I'd give you the world if I could," she whispered.

She knew she couldn't give the baby the world, but she could give it a family.

A father.

For the last three months she'd planned on raising this child alone, and now she'd found its father. How on earth was she going to tell Michael? What would his reaction be?

She knew that as the heir to the throne, having an illegitimate child would be difficult.

Beyond difficult.

Impossible.

Maybe they could tell people Michael was the baby's godfather, as a way of explaining why he spent time with her child. A benevolent godfather.

It would be good for his image, would allow him to bond with his child, and would keep the baby from becoming fodder for the paparazzi.

Of course, everyone would have questions about the baby's father. She was trying to come up with an explanation when there was a knock on her door.

She wished she could ignore it and just sit here reveling in the fact that her baby moved. But whoever it was knocked again.

"Coming," she said, getting off the bed and walking reluctantly toward the door.

She opened it. Oh, no. "Your Highness. What did you want?"

Michael didn't wait for an invitation. He simply walked past her and right into the room.

"We need to talk," he said.

"There's nothing to talk about."

He flopped—flopped in a very unprincely fashion—into a chair. Cara was pretty sure Miss Manners would say that even a prince should wait to be invited before making himself comfortable in a lady's bedroom.

"Make yourself at home," she said with more than a touch of sarcasm in her voice.

Shey would be so proud. She'd been trying to teach Cara the fine art of sarcasm since they started college. With that little comment, Cara thought she'd finally begun to make progress. Okay, so it had only taken eight years, but it was finally a step forward.

Michael surveyed the room. "I take it you've settled in?"

Cara quickly scanned the room. Nothing was out of place, all her belongings were carefully stored. "It appears I have. I congratulate you on stating the obvious."

He ignored her second attempt at sarcasm, though she thought it was a pretty good jab.

"You've been avoiding me," he said instead.

She couldn't think of anything to say to that, sarcastic or otherwise. She settled for saying, "I see you every night at dinner. And when you tag along on outings, or help your mother and me with plans."

"Surrounded by my family and assorted friends. That's not what I had in mind."

If Michael wasn't a prince and she'd found him, discovered he'd been looking for her, she might be able to think of something to say, but he was a prince, and she wasn't capable of thinking of anything, so it seemed to her that saying nothing was better.

"Have you thought about me?" he asked softly. "About that night?"

Every day, she thought, but she said, "Sorry. No."

"I've thought of you almost every waking hour. And since I haven't slept well since that night we shared, there have been more waking hours than normal. The few hours I do manage to sleep, I dream of you. Trying to find you consumed me. And now that I have found you—"

"To be honest, you didn't find me."

"Now that I know where you are," he corrected, "it hasn't gotten any better. I still can't sleep. Knowing you're so close, but still so far away. Too far away."

"You know most men would be embarrassed to admit a one-night stand stayed on their mind beyond that one night."

"I'm not most men," he told her, no bragging, no apologies.

"You can say that again," she muttered.

Not quite sarcasm, but a good try nonetheless. But she knew he was right…. There was nothing ordinary about Michael. Even before she'd known he was a prince, she'd known that.

"I gave you time to get settled. I didn't want to cause you any more stress. Especially since I'm not wholly convinced you're okay. But now that you've settled in, maybe you'd consider having dinner with me tomorrow night? We could talk and—"

"Listen, Michael—Your Highness—I'm here to do a job. As soon as that job's done, I'm leaving. There will be no replays of what happened three months ago, no passionate reunion. That night wasn't me. I don't do things like that. The truth of the matter is, I was lonely. My two friends had fallen in love, and I'd watched it happen. I was happy for them, but I felt so utterly alone. The odd man out. Looking back, it was silly. Shey and Parker may have found their soul mates, but they're still my best friends, still there for me. But that night, I was adrift, wishing for my own soul mate."

"And you found me." He looked far too pleased at the thought.

"Yes, I found you. But Michael, it could have been anybody." She realized, even as she said the words, that they were a lie. There was something about Michael that even now, when she knew better, called to her.

"Listen," she continued, "for those few precious hours we spent together I allowed myself to believe you were something you weren't, that we had something we can never have."

"Why? Why can't we have the kind of love that your friends have found?" he asked.

"You're a prince, and I'm...I'm just me. Cara Phillips. Reserved, bookish. Ordinary. Let's just leave that one night in the past, a beautiful dream. Because that's all it was, a dream. Insubstantial. Unable to hold its form in the bright light of day."

Michael looked as if he were going to argue, but then stopped himself. He stood and said, "We'll talk some more tomorrow."

"I'm sure we'll talk, Your Highness. But it will be social talk. No mention of that night. I've said all that needs to be said."

Except she hadn't told him about the baby.

She tried to say the words, but they wouldn't come. How did you tell a man he was going to be a father.

Michael, about that night...oops.

No, she was sure that wouldn't work, but wasn't sure what would.

Later.

She'd tell him later. After the wedding. For now, she needed more time to think through the ramifications of carrying the child of a prince.

She stood and opened the door.

Michael didn't oblige. As a matter of fact, he stood there, giving her a look that made her feel decidedly uncomfortable.

It made her feel naked. Not in an undressed sort of way, but rather in a he-could-see-into-her-very-soul sort of way.

The studious look was suddenly replaced by another. A hungry sort of look.

"Stop that," she said, wanting to give him a small push out the door, but hesitant to actually touch him. The memories of all their touches that night still haunted her. She wasn't sure she could even afford a small, casual touch.

"Stop what?" he asked.

"Giving me a big-bad-wolf-about-to-eat-Red-Riding-Hood sort of look."

"What sort of look?" he asked, chuckling.

Seeing amusement in his eyes was definitely an improvement over the other two looks. Yes, humor was better than studious or hungry.

"Okay," she said, unable to resist a small smile. "So maybe I've read at too many story times for the eight-and-under crowd. My analogies could use some work."

"I liked your analogy just fine. As a matter of fact, come here, Red Riding Hood and let me show you my big, bad…"

He let the sentence trail off and that hungry look was back. Cara felt especially Red-Riding-Hoodish. Knowing she should run and escape, but wondering just what this particular wolf was about to do.

He moved toward her in slow motion. Easy, as if he if thought she might bolt.

Cara could have told him that there was no way she could move even if she wanted to. She knew she should want to, but she wasn't sure she did.

"Cara mia," he murmured just before his lips touched hers.

The same jolt that had shaken her from her usual staid manner three months ago hit her again. It zapped every ounce of common sense from her brain. That had to be why, rather than pulling away, she stepped into his embrace.

It had to be the explanation for her arms wrapping around his neck of their own volition.

It had to be why she was the one to deepen the kiss, the one to pull him closer, the one to hold on as if she never wanted to let go.

That jolt had burned her synapses and her brain could no longer control her body.

Michael was the one to break off the kiss. He was back to studying her again. His index finger brushed against her lips.

"Do you still maintain there's nothing between us?" he asked, his voice hoarse.

Cara didn't know how to answer. She'd fibbed to him about that night, and thought she'd done a pretty good job of it, but lying now would only make her look absurd. So she ignored the question and simply said, "Good night, Michael." She held the door open for him.

"But Cara—"

She didn't allow him to finish his *but Cara*. Instead she repeated, "Good night."

He sighed and walked from the room. "You can lie to yourself, but you can't lie to me after you kissed me like that. There's still something there, and I think it's getting bigger."

Cara shut the door and sighed her relief, knowing it was just a temporary respite.

The only thing they had between them was a baby, and Michael was right, it was getting bigger. Soon she wouldn't be able to hide it anymore.

Truth be told, she didn't want to hide it.

Even though Michael being a prince complicated things more than they already were, it didn't alter the fact that Cara wanted this baby. She loved it. And she couldn't wait to share the news with her friends.

But first she had to share the news with Michael.

Less than three more weeks, she told herself firmly. All she had to do was hang in until after the wedding, then she could go home to her normal life.

Her hand rested on her stomach. Maybe not so normal.

Her mind was far too muddled to figure out anything tonight.

Maybe tomorrow, things would be clearer.

Michael felt buoyed by his success. Not only had he kissed Cara, she'd kissed him back. No one could fake that kind of desire.

She wanted him as much as he wanted her.

So why was she holding back?

Marstel startled Michael from his thoughts. "How did it go?"

"I finally talked to her…alone."

Rather than being sympathetic to his plight, his friend laughed. "The great Prince Michael, reduced to cornering women. What is the world coming to?"

"It's not funny, Marstel," Michael said, warning in his voice.

Marstel didn't have a warning meter. He never knew when he was pushing the limits.

"Actually it is quite funny," he assured Michael. "I didn't laugh at all when you spent three months looking for your mystery woman, so I feel I'm allowed a couple chuckles now that you found her and she's making you work for it."

"Some friend."

"Do you want to go over your schedule?"

Michael didn't think he could concentrate on anything but Cara. "Later maybe?"

They walked in companionable silence for a minute, then Marstel asked, "Is she still mad that you left her?"

"I didn't leave her, she left me." Michael shook his head. "No, that's not fair either. Our losing each other was a mix-up."

"So now that you've found each other, why aren't you unmixing?"

"Things are even worse. I don't know why she's trying to deny what's between us, but I know things will straighten themselves out eventually. She might not want to admit it, but she's my destiny."

"The question is," Marstel said quietly, "are you her destiny? She doesn't seem to think so."

"She's wrong."

They walked without saying anything more for a while longer, then Marstel suddenly blurted out, "She might think you're not her destiny, but she watches you all the time."

"All what time?" Michael asked.

"At dinner. Every night."

"She doesn't watch me, she just talks wedding plans with my mother and visits with the ambassador."

"She looks, all right," Marstel assured him. "Whenever you're not looking she's watching you with the intensity of someone on a diet looking at a piece of chocolate cake."

Michael laughed. Marstel's current girlfriend was continually dieting, and they'd all seen her chocolate-hungry look.

"And," Marstel continued, "there's something in her eyes that makes me think she feels more for you than she wants to let on."

"Why would she try to hide it?"

Marstel shrugged. "You can be sure I don't understand women. I don't even try."

"No, you simply pack up and move on when things get tough."

"That's right," Marstel said with a nod. "And if I were talking to anyone but you, I'd suggest you do the same."

"But you wouldn't suggest it to me? Why?" Michael asked.

"Because you're an arrogant prince who doesn't listen to anybody's advice but your own."

Marstel had known him a long time, but obviously didn't know him as well as he thought he did. "You're wrong. I listen to suggestions all day."

"Ah," Marstel murmured, nodding his head. "Suggestions and advice for the country. But not for your personal life."

"I—" Michael knew he couldn't argue.

Marstel had been suggesting, not so subtly, that he give up the search for his mystery woman since he'd started it. But Michael knew that he was meant to be with Cara. No one could have talked him out of it.

There was no arguing with the fact, so he didn't even try. And he was saved from changing the subject when his mobile rang. He pulled it out of his pocket and glanced at the caller ID.

"I have to take this," he said.

"Saved by the bell," Marstel said, grinning as he gave a wave and walked down the hall.

"Hello," Michael said to Jace, his future brother-in-law and private investigator.

"I got your message about calling off the search. Are you sure?"

"Positive," Michael said.

For a moment he thought about telling Jace that he'd found his Cara, but he decided to hold off for a while. This prickly Cara was trying to run from what they had. He wouldn't give her another reason to avoid him by telling her friends and annoying her.

"I'm sorry," Jace said. "Are you going to be okay? I know how much this meant to you."

"I'll be fine," Michael assured him. They continued to talk about this and that, and Michael realized he was right. He'd be fine as soon as he could convince Cara that they were destined for one another.

Four

"So, young lady, why the long face?"

Cara jumped at the sound of a voice. She'd thought she'd found the perfect hiding place. A little sitting nook, tucked in a seldom-used corridor. She'd been trying to avoid Michael since that kiss a few days ago. Thankfully, it wasn't Michael who'd discovered her, but Ambassador McClinnon.

"I'm fine, sir. How was your day?"

He took a seat across from her. "Paul and I went fishing this morning. He doesn't relax enough. When I visit I'm under the queen's orders to see to it he does. Anna might not have been born a royal, but she does have the regal command mastered."

"And did it work today?" she asked.

She loved Parker's parents. They were hardworking advocates for Eliason.

"He didn't catch a gol-darned thing, but he did spend a lot of time laughing, so I'm thinking it did."

Every now and again a hint of the ambassador's southern roots slipped into his voice.

"Garn-darned?" she asked, smiling at the term.

He chuckled. "Sometimes there aren't any swearwords like the ones of your youth."

Cara looked up from the seating chart she was working on.

Actually reworking.

She'd come up with a version based on Shey and Parker's suggestions, and now was trying to incorporate the queen's personal assistant Esme's suggestions as well. She felt like she was walking a tightrope, trying to keep everyone happy.

"Did you know that you can't sit Parker's godmother near her great-uncle Sven because back in the day they had a fling?" she asked.

He smiled warmly. "The heart is a fickle thing. It can carry a torch or carry a grudge for decades. Love and hate, it's a fine line."

"I can't imagine carrying a grudge against anyone I loved."

"Then you're a rare lady," he said with a wistful note in his voice.

"You can imagine someone who can?"

"Let me tell you a little story. When I was more than a bit younger, there was this girl at home. I fell in love with her in kindergarten. We got caught snitching cookies and sat in the corner together. I couldn't imagine a life without her. She was my everything."

The ambassador got lost for a moment in the memory of his girl.

"What happened?" Cara finally asked.

"We had a volatile relationship all through school. We fought, we made up. The making up was especially sweet. One time after a fight, she was working a kissing booth and I paid to kiss her…. Oh, how we made up that time."

Lightly his finger brushed his lip, as if he could remember the feel of that kiss all these years later.

"Where is she now?" Cara asked.

"One fight, we didn't make up. I was waiting for her to apologize. I guess she was waiting for me to, as well. All I know is one day she was gone and it was too late. I left and went to graduate school and her family all moved away. I came home and she was gone."

He paused a moment. "How on earth did I start talking about Pearly?"

"Pearly?" Cara asked weakly.

Cara's bookstore back in Erie, Pennsylvania, was located on Perry Square. Right across the park there was a beauty salon, Snips and Snaps, where the square's version of a town crier, Pearly Gates, worked.

The ambassador's Pearly couldn't be the same one. But for the life of her, Cara couldn't imagine two Pearlys roaming the U.S.

"Pearly Gates. Oh, that girl was a pistol. Kept a fella on his toes. She's probably long since married, with a house full of kids and grandkids. Pearly was the type who needed a family."

"Pearly Gates?" she murmured more to herself than to the ambassador.

"I know, it's an unusual name. She used to say her mama named her Pearly Gates to remind herself that her daughter came from heaven. Her mama, and the rest of the world, needed the reminder because Pearly had a bit of the devil in her."

Cara's suspicion was confirmed.

She'd heard Pearly tell that very story. Pearly's childhood sweetheart here in Eliason… Who would have thought?

But Cara knew that the ambassador was wrong. Pearly had never married, never had that house full of kids and grandkids. But she did have a family. A large extended one that encompassed all of Perry Square. Pearly was truly the square's heart.

"She sounds like something special," Cara said. More than sounded. Cara knew firsthand just how special Pearly was.

And she was coming to Eliason for the wedding.

Cara thought about telling the ambassador, but decided against it. She'd let them both be surprised.

"Oh, she was special," he said, wistfully. "I've often wondered where she is now. Her whole family scattered to the four corners of the earth it seems."

"And here you are in Eliason, the friend of a king."

"Yes, it sometimes still feels surreal. Back then I

was just Buster McClinnon and I planned on being with Pearly forever."

He suddenly gave himself a little shake and stood. "I apologize. You were sitting enjoying a quiet space to work in, and I came and interrupted with an old man's remembrances."

"It's too bad all my interruptions weren't as pleasant," Cara assured him.

"Forgive my interference, but I wondered if you needed any assistance."

"I'll figure this seating chart out, but thanks."

"Not with that, with Michael. I've noticed you playing hide-and-seek with the prince."

"I don't know what you mean," she said as a sinking feeling hit her. If Ambassador McClinnon had noticed, then who else noticed?

"Your secret's safe with me. I think everyone else is so wrapped up in the wedding plans that they haven't seen that something's going on between the two of you."

Before she could deny it, he said, "And there is something. Do you want to talk about it?"

"Not right now, but thank you."

"Any time my dear. Any time." The ambassador slowly walked away, and Cara thought she heard him murmur, *Pearly.*

Cara didn't want to think about what the ambassador had said. She wasn't even sure how they'd moved from discussing seating charts to love.

The ability to turn a conversation…Pearly Gates had it as well.

It was easier to think about reuniting Pearly and the ambassador at the wedding than to think about her problems. So she made a quick call to Parker, filled her in on the wedding plans and then on finding Pearly's love.

"I've known Ambassador McClinnon all my life. You're sure he meant our Pearly?"

"Positive. There couldn't be two Pearly Gates in the country."

"In the whole world," Parker added.

They both laughed and then Parker launched into one of her Jace-itis attacks. She gushed and raved about her fiancé, about their plans. Cara had learned just to let the attacks run their course. An occasional *oh,* or *really* was all it took to keep Parker going.

Shey was known to have Tanner-itis on occasion, but she didn't seem to gush nearly as much as Parker. But the fact that Shey gushed at all showed the true depth of her feelings.

"Oh, hey, Jace is here," Parker said. "I've got to run."

"No problem. Just wanted to let you know about Pearly and keep you up-to-date on the plans."

"Thanks, Cara. Not just for the call, but for everything."

"You know I'd do anything for you and Shey."

"The feeling's mutual," Parker said.

Cara had tears in her eyes as she hung up. She'd read that pregnant women were more emotional, but she'd never expected this.

She wiped her face and started gathering up her papers.

"*Cara mia,* what's wrong?"

"Oh, jeez. You shouldn't sneak up on people like that." She jumped to her feet, wiped at her eyes again and tried to do a circumspect sniff.

So much for her quiet hideaway. Tomorrow she'd have to hunt a new one out.

That was the good thing about the castle—there were a lot of nooks and crannies.

"I didn't sneak," he said. "A prince never sneaks. You were just too preoccupied with your crying to hear me approach."

"I wasn't crying."

He trailed a finger down her left cheek and held it out for her to inspect. It was obviously damp.

"My eyes were watering," she said. "Allergies, I think."

"What are you allergic to?" he asked, not appearing to believe her.

"Princes."

Oh, that was good. She was keeping track of all her best comebacks to share with Shey. She was doing her friend proud.

"Really?" Michael asked. "You didn't seem allergic when I did this…."

Cara knew what he was going to do, just like she knew she should run. But she simply stood there and waited, a shot of anticipation coursing through her body as he pulled her into his arms.

"Not allergies," he whispered softly against her

neck. "I wish you'd tell me what's wrong. If it's possible, I'll fix it."

"I don't need anyone to fix my problems." First Parker, now Michael. "I'm an adult, and I'm totally capable of addressing my own problems. The only thing I need right now is a good allergy pill."

"Cara mia." That's all he said, just that absurd pet name she'd found so endearing that first night and now grated on her every last nerve.

Okay, so maybe it didn't always grate as much as it should. Right now, as a matter of fact, it felt sort of sweet.

He kissed her softly on the cheek, and, needing to put some space between them, she took a step back.

The kiss, rather than comforting her, only left her hungry for more.

He grabbed her arm softly and held her in place, then pulled her gently toward him. She could have pulled away, should have, but she didn't.

"Cara mia," he murmured as his lips touched hers.

This kiss didn't have the hunger the other one had. It was soft and spoke of understanding and empathy.

It melted the last of Cara's resistance.

She wanted this man even though she knew it was too soon to feel anything but a superficial attraction. She knew it in her head, but couldn't seem to convince her heart of anything but the fact she wanted him. Wanted him with a growing passion she didn't know how to extinguish.

As if it knew, the baby fluttered again.

Just a small brush, as soft as Cara imagined a butterfly's wings would be. She pulled back from Michael and her hand flew to her stomach.

For a moment she almost reached for Michael's hand, to place it on the baby…their baby. But that moment was fleeting and she remembered he didn't know yet.

"Cara?" he asked, staring at her—studying her. This time it was far more intense than it ever had been before.

The time had come. She faced the inevitable and said, "Michael, we have to talk."

She had to tell him and now was as good a time as any.

"I've been saying we have to talk for almost a week while you played your little seek and hide."

"Hide-and-seek," she corrected.

He just glared. "Played your games. Is it mine?"

"What?" She was sure she'd heard wrong. Michael couldn't be asking what she thought he was asking. But he was staring at her stomach as if she had some big belly-button ring poking out.

"You're pregnant," he said flatly. "Is it mine?"

"I—" Her first impulse was to deny she was pregnant, even though she'd been just about to tell him.

She didn't.

Instead she asked, "What on earth would make you say such a thing?"

"Three months," he said with certainty. "I can do the math. You're three months along. When were you going to tell me? Or *were* you going to tell me?"

"Why would I tell you? I've been dating a man named…" She paused a moment and then blurted out the first male name she could latch onto, "Stuart."

She'd been reading E. B. White's *Stuart Little* to the kids at Titles' story time before she'd left Erie. Stuart was a good name.

"Ha."

Michael wasn't buying it. That much was clear.

Cara felt a bit insulted. After all, was it so hard to believe that another man might have found her attractive enough to date? "You don't think someone else would be interested in me?" She didn't have to fake the annoyance in her voice.

How dare the conceited *prince* feel as if once a woman had known him she was ruined for all other men.

Okay, so it might be true—was true—but still, if he thought so, it just made his swollen head seem almost too swollen for him to get his crown on.

Not that she'd ever seen him in a crown.

Still she was sure he had one and at the rate his ego was growing…

"There is no Stuart." Michael didn't look quite as sure of himself.

"Well, I call him Stu for short. He's a nice man. A normal, home-by-five-every-night sort of man."

"What does this Stuart do for a living?"

"He's a…" Again she scrambled for an answer. "A professor at Gannon. That's how we met."

She was warming up to the fictional Stuart. He had no royal baggage, no hang-ups at all. He was perfect for her. "He came into Monarch's and Titles for coffee and a book. We started talking, and before long we were dating. We're still dating."

"You're doing more than dating if this baby's his. How far along are you?"

"Thr—" She almost blurted out three months, but caught herself.

"Just barely," she said instead.

"Why won't you just admit the truth? I know there's no Professor Stu."

She should have thought of this before. Stuart was the perfect out. Her idea of Michael being the baby's benevolent godfather would still work. He wouldn't have to deal with the scandal of having an illegitimate baby.

"Put yourself in my place," she said gently. "You're a prince. Royalty. Something I'm not. Think about what it would be like if this were your baby, not that I'm admitting that," she added hastily. "You have to think this through. *If* this baby were yours— and I'm not saying it is—but if the baby were yours, it wouldn't just affect you and me, it would affect your people. You have obligations that have to take precedence. I may not be royal, but I'm pretty sure a prince can't have an illegitimate baby."

"Which is why we'll get married."

Cara didn't mean to, but she snorted a *ha* that was even more emphatic than the one he'd used about her fictional Stuart.

"I don't think so," she assured him. "Again, you're a prince, I own a bookstore. You can't marry me. Think of the country."

"There are any number of things I'll do for my country, for my people. Who I marry is something I won't let them dictate."

"What about your parents? What would they say?"

She could only imagine their disappointment and disapproval. She didn't want to cause them either— she genuinely liked Michael and Parker's parents.

"They already love you."

"Then what about me? Don't you think I deserve something more than being the woman you *had to* marry?"

"I was looking for you—"

She cut him off. "Michael, you have to think about this. Think long and hard. Weigh all the options. Whatever happens next will affect more people than just us."

"What did Parker say?" he asked.

"About the baby?" She shook her head. "I haven't told her. Haven't told anyone but my doctors."

"You didn't tell Parker?" He sounded surprised.

"At first I didn't say anything to her and Shey because I didn't want to take any of the attention from their weddings. I planned to tell them after their honeymoons."

"And when were you going to tell me?"

"Not you, Stuart."

Gently, so gently it was almost her undoing, he

brushed a finger down her cheek. "*Cara mia,* I understand your fears and concerns. We'll work through them. But I know in my heart that this is our baby, that there is no Stuart. This baby was conceived on the most magical night of my life."

"When we kissed, the baby moved," she found herself blurting out.

She wasn't admitting there was no Stuart, or that the baby was Michael's, at least not until he gave the situation some thought. But she longed—no, needed—to share it with him.

"It's kicking now?" he asked.

"No kicking," she said. "Just moving. Small flutters. You can't feel it outside yet, but inside, I can feel it."

"Our baby." He reached his hand toward her, and for a moment she thought he was going to caress her stomach, but the moment passed and his hand fell back.

"I need to think about this," he stated.

"Yes, you do. In the end, you'll realize that there's your duty to your country and to your family, that has to be your priority. I promise you that this baby will never know a moment of want, of need. This baby is already loved."

"Cara," he started but then just shook his head and walked away.

Yeah. That went well.

Cara felt tears well up again.

Damned allergies.

Five

Michael smiled and waved at the crowd, but even as he went through the motions of opening the new hospital wing, his mind swirled around what he'd learned.

A father.

He was going to be a father.

Michael rolled the idea over and over in his mind but couldn't quite get beyond the shock.

"We'd like to welcome our prince…" the hospital director droned.

Michael knew that, despite what Cara claimed, this was his baby—their baby—just as he'd known the moment he met her that Cara was his destiny.

Now she'd come back to him and they were going to be parents.

Marstel elbowed him and he realized it was his turn to talk. He tried to concentrate on remembering his speech. "I'd like to thank you all for coming out today. But more than that, I'd like to thank you all for your support and donations…."

He fell into the rhythm of the speech. He'd made public appearances all his life. He'd given his first speech at the age of fifteen. This was a role he was at home with.

But, father?

He was going to be someone's father.

So many emotions jangled through his head. Fear. Wondering if he could do it, if he could juggle a very public life with the very private role of father.

Anticipation. He couldn't wait to meet his son or daughter.

Love.

Overriding all his other emotions there was love. His child.

There was nothing he wouldn't do for it.

Him.

Her.

His baby.

And it moved when he kissed Cara. As if it knew he was its father.

He hated calling the baby *it*.

Weren't there tests to discover what the baby's gender was? Maybe Cara knew. Maybe he should go find her and see.

But no. She was still claiming there was a *Stuart* in the picture. Michael didn't believe it for a minute, but he could understand why she'd created her decoy-dad.

Marrying into a royal family wouldn't be a piece of cake.

He finished his speech, then took a ceremonial pair of oversize scissors from the hospital director and cut the ribbon, officially opening the new cardiac unit.

He nodded and shook hands as he made his way through the crowd. Another ceremonial duty attended to. It was just another facet of his life.

But not everyone was cut out for this life.

Look at Parker—she'd been born into it and wanted nothing to do with being scrutinized by the media, having each action, each decision weighed and judged. But somehow he knew Cara would realize it was worth it in the end.

That he was worth it.

He was positive she'd figure it out.

Well, *almost* positive.

Actually, the sinking feeling in the pit of his stomach just might be something less than positive.

It might be something akin to fear.

What if Cara didn't figure out that what they had was worth any difficulties that came along with being royalty?

What would the paparazzi make of her? She was pregnant and unwed. He was a prince, destined to be king.

They would have a field day.

What if she wouldn't weather that sort of media frenzy and left?

How could he be a father to the baby if she went back to Erie?

This baby would need a father, and he knew there was no Professor Stu waiting in the wings. This was his baby.

Again, he wished he knew if it was a boy or girl, and decided that for now he'd just think of it as the baby.

His baby.

"Michael," Marstel said loudly, with more than a tinge of impatience.

Michael realized they'd cleared the crowd and were headed toward the exit.

"Sorry. I was just thinking."

"I could see the smoke as those wheels ground together. What's wrong?"

"I—" He wanted to shout out to his friend, to the whole world, that he was going to be a father. But he knew he had to wait and settle things with Cara first.

Most especially they had to resolve the whole Stuart question.

"Nothing's wrong," he said.

They climbed into the limo and the security got into a sedan behind them.

Marstel did a nice grimace and head-shake of disbelief as the limo started back to the castle. "I didn't need to ask what was wrong. I know exactly what it is…. It's her. You've been wrapped tight since she arrived. Face it, the woman doesn't want to renew your relationship."

"That's what I thought, but now I'm not so sure. We've kissed twice."

Marstel looked surprised. "I thought you couldn't find her, what with the way she's been hiding from you?"

"How dare you doubt your prince," Michael teased. "I did find her and we did kiss. And it's still there. That spark we had three months ago. The only difference is it's grown larger."

Cara was going to grow larger.

Michael imagined her stomach rounding, his baby growing inside and something in him spoke to him. "As a matter of fact, I'd like you to do something for me."

"What?"

Michael laid out his plan and Marstel nodded. "Wine or champagne?"

"Neither," Michael said. "Cara doesn't drink. Sparkling grape juice will be fine."

He knew pregnant women couldn't drink, but what other accommodations did they need to make? What else did they need to be careful of?

All of a sudden he realized how much he didn't know about pregnancy.

"All right. I'll have it all ready by seven," Marstel assured him. "Where do you want it? Your rooms?"

Michael doubted Cara would come talk in his private wing of the castle, and tried to think of a private, more neutral place. "On the roof."

That was perfect. Fresh air. He might not know

as much as he wanted to know about pregnancy, but he was pretty sure pregnant women should have plenty of fresh air.

Marstel smiled. "It's good to see you're done moping and are going after what you want."

"I'm not just going after her, I'm going to win her." He was going to take care of her and take care of their baby starting here and now.

"Now, if you'll excuse me, I have some reading I need to get done."

When they arrived at the castle, he hurried toward his office. He doubted they had any baby books lying around, but he was sure there would be information on the Internet.

Cara finished the menu discussion with the queen and Marta, the cook Tommy had mentioned. The woman was actually a five-star chef. A sweet woman who'd blushed when Cara mentioned Tommy had spoken of her.

Maybe Marta really did have a crush on the doctor.

She was smiling at the notion as they called it a day.

"We'll pick this up in the morning then?" the queen said.

"I'll meet you in your office about eight," Cara assured her.

"Are you sure you'll be all right on your own for dinner tonight?" the queen asked with motherly concern.

"I'll be fine. A quiet night is just what I need."

"Then I'll say good-night now, and see you in the morning." She gave Cara a brief kiss on the forehead and left.

As Cara made her way into the hall where her room was located, Michael's assistant was waiting. He handed Cara a note, then hastily made his escape.

When she opened it and read, *Meet me on the roof, Michael,* she knew why Marstel had been in such a hurry to leave.

Short, Terse. An order.

Cara tried to tamp down the burning in her stomach as she glanced at the small map that was guiding her to the proper staircase.

She went in her room and slammed the door.

Tamping wasn't working. The burning flamed for the umpteenth time.

The arrogant, thinks-he-rules-the-world prince thought he could just order her and she'd do as she was told?

Just who did he think he was to boss her around?

Actually, the answer was pretty clear. Michael thought he was a prince because, truth be told, he was.

But still, the roof?

Cara didn't know what to make of that.

It got even stranger when he'd added a postscript to his royal, bossy decree. *Dress to the nines.*

You dressed to the nines for dates, and she was definitely not dating Michael.

So the nines were out. She knew that the minute she read the command.

However, even though she wasn't dating Michael, it didn't mean she couldn't be neat and tidy. The problem was deciding how dressed was dressed enough, but not quite what he asked for.

No, not asked, commanded.

After agonizing for a ridiculous amount of time in front of her closet's contents, she finally decided a *seven* was neat and tidy, but definitely wasn't a *nine*.

And she had decided her plain black sheath dress was simply neat, tidy and seven-ish. Definitely not nine-ish.

And the pearls?

Well, her grandmother had left them to her and they weren't so much to spice the dress up, but simply a reminder that she was loved.

If the dress hadn't suddenly become more snug than normal, it might have even made an eight. But sevens and eights weren't nines, so Michael wouldn't assume she'd dressed for a date.

Cara decided she was a well-dressed, prompt navigational goddess when she found herself walking up the stairs at six fifty-nine.

She'd have to tell Michael the truth tonight. He'd have realized by now that he couldn't claim the baby as his. They could keep Stu as a public cover.

She wasn't sure why she'd made him up. Professor Stu.

Fear maybe?

Actually, no *maybe* about it.

She was scared. She'd had time to adjust to the

idea of carrying a baby, of being a mother. Well, adjust as much as any pregnant woman could. She couldn't wait for her baby to arrive.

But finding Michael, and finding out her baby's father was a prince? It was going to take longer than just one short week to adjust to that.

Longer than the rest of her pregnancy, she was pretty sure.

Still, he deserved the truth. Together they'd work out what would be best for all of them.

"Hello?" she called as she opened the door. The roof was dark.

Maybe she'd gotten the directions wrong? Maybe there was another section of roof where she was supposed to be. Goodness knows this place was big enough to have any number of roof sections.

"Hello?" she called again.

Lights snapped on.

Tiny white lights, like the kind she used on her own Christmas tree, twinkled in the small trees and hedges that lined the perimeter of the large, flat roof.

A small flash of more light from the center of the roof caught her eye. There he was.

Michael was lighting candles that were gracing an elaborately set table.

He was dressed in a tux and wasn't merely a nine. He was a ten. An eleven even.

"Michael?" she said.

He smiled at her and simply said, "I've been waiting for you, Cara. Come in."

"Said the spider to the fly," she muttered as she moved toward the table.

She knew she should leave, that she needed a clear head to figure out what to do about Michael and that whatever he had planned was bound to do anything but clear things up.

Yes, this looked like a muddy-the-waters sort of evening if ever she'd seen one.

"Have a seat," he said, pulling the chair out with old-world chivalry.

"What on earth is this, Michael? I was hoping you'd come to your senses and simply wanted to talk."

"We can talk as we eat, right?" Michael smiled again, the picture of innocence.

"Don't *dinner* me, Your Highness," Cara said. "You're up to something."

"What on earth could I be up to?" He took the seat across from her and smiled again.

It was a smile that a cat might use after it had swallowed the canary. But Michael was about to learn that Cara was no bird to be had.

"What could you be up to? I don't know. Maybe, this." She gestured to the ultra-romantic setting.

"This?" he repeated, as if he didn't have a clue in the world what she could possibly be talking about.

"This is *Dinner* with a capital *D*. Something you'd plan to impress a woman. We're here to discuss…" She paused. "Things."

"Our baby," he supplied.

Tell him.

Tell him, a voice in her head urged.

Say the words *our baby.* Confirm that it's his baby and that Professor Stuart was just a figment of your overly active imagination.

"And, there's another pressing matter we need to discuss." He poured something into her wineglass. "It's just sparkling grape juice," he assured her.

"What other pressing matter?" She took a sip of the liquid.

"Our baby and our wedding, of course."

"Wedding?" she squeaked.

He'd had time to think about the situation and surely he realized they couldn't marry.

The look in his eyes said more clearly than words that he didn't realize any such thing.

"*My* baby," she said, standing.

There would be no retiring the professor tonight. Stuart would just have to stick around a bit longer.

"Our baby," he said again, with a smile. He put some puffy-looking pastry thing on her plate.

"Sit down before you fall down. Please," he said.

Cara sat, not because she liked being told what to do, even if he did say please, but because he was right, she was feeling a bit shaky on her feet.

"Listen," she said. "I'm sorry if the truth hurts your feelings, but there is a Stuart at home."

That wasn't really a lie. She was sure there was a Stuart somewhere within the Erie city limits.

"He's a good man," she added.

Not so much a lie either. There had to be a good Stuart somewhere in Erie.

But for the next part she crossed her fingers firmly. "I met him the day after you left me—"

"I didn't leave you." Michael was frowning now. "I came back with your breakfast and you were gone. A misunderstanding. I thought we settled that."

She uncrossed her fingers and looked him full in the eyes. "I'm sorry. We did."

She was sorry for so much more than that. Sorry that Michael wasn't just some ordinary man. Although, before she'd even known he was a prince, she'd known he was extraordinary.

"Really," she said, "I am sorry."

His expression softened. "Now, let's settle the rest of it."

"I don't know what you mean," she said, though she did. Another lie. Once you told that first one, it was a slippery slope.

"Our baby," he said.

"My baby." Michael wasn't thinking straight or he wouldn't be so obstinate. She was giving him the perfect out, the fictional Stuart.

She'd tell him the truth later when he realized that his responsibility was with his country. For now, it was up to her to protect him when he wouldn't protect himself. She cared about him too much to see his reputation suffer.

"*Cara mia,* there is no Stuart, some wimpy boy—"

"Professor," she interrupted, feeling insulted on the fictitious Stuart's behalf.

"Professor," he corrected, sneering the word. "Some wimpy professor-boy who claimed your affections."

"Not a boy. A man. All man. A manly man. Not a wimpy bone in his body."

She waited to see jealousy on his face, but instead there was laughter.

"What?" she asked.

"Cara, that night was your first time, so I know you're not one to share your affections lightly. Which would lead me to believe you're also not one to move from my bed directly into someone else's. The baby is mine. What I don't understand is why you're denying it."

"I've told you, you're a prince," she said, feeling utterly defeated. "I've known Parker long enough to know a lot about you. You're your father's heir. Heir to a throne, to a kingdom. You can't go around having children out of wedlock."

"You're right I can't."

"So, there's Stuart. My big, manly, burly professor who wooed me with his brilliant mind."

"Or, we could marry as soon as possible. I had hoped we could elope tonight after dinner."

It was as if every breath she'd taken since coming onto the roof whooshed out in one swift exhale.

For a moment she wondered if she'd forgotten how to inhale. She couldn't seem to draw any oxygen back in. The room started spinning, and suddenly she remembered. She inhaled and exhaled a couple more times for good measure, then said, "Pardon me?"

"Marriage," he said slowly. "It makes sense, *cara mia*. For us. For our baby. Come away with me tonight and make me an honest man."

"You've got to be kidding. I would never get married because I have to. When I marry I want what Parker and Shey have found."

"And you don't think you can find that with me?" He sounded hurt.

Hurting Michael wasn't her intent, but marrying him? Eloping tonight?

She meant what she said—when she married she wanted the whole nine yards. A man who loved her. A man she loved.

She knew she felt something for Michael. Something that pulled at her. Something more than she'd ever felt for any man. But love?

They simply hadn't known each other long enough for it to be love.

And until she could find what her two friends had found, she'd remain single and raise this baby alone.

"Michael, Parker adores you and thinks the world of you. Even though you're her brother, she wouldn't care so much if you weren't a nice guy, but—"

"*But*. I hate that word. Nothing good has ever come after a *but*."

"But," she said again, "the truth is, we don't know each other well enough. We certainly don't…" She paused, not wanting to use the *L* word, even as a denial of the way they felt. "Don't have the same feelings that Parker and Shey have found with Jace and Tanner."

Michael shook his head. "What we had was an immediate spark, a connection on a primal level. And that one night, the spark grew to something more. When I saw you at the airport, it blazed back to life, bigger, brighter than ever before."

"You were imagining things," she protested.

It was easier to believe that than to admit she felt the spark as well.

"No," Michael insisted. "I wasn't imagining anything. In my family we fall hard and fast. We know when we've met the right person. Look at my sister and Jace, at how quick that was. All I had to do was see her in person and hear her talk about him to know it was meant to be."

"That's different."

"No. I was coming to look for you as soon as the wedding was over. Back in Erie, I had to leave that next day, I had duties. But Jace was looking for you, and like I said, I was coming back. I've been crazy, wondering where you were, what you were doing. Wondering who you were. Do you know how much it hurt that I didn't even know your name? That night, you were just my *cara mia,* but in the light of day, I couldn't wait to learn everything about you. To know your name, who you were, what you wanted."

"You did know my name, after all." She remembered how his casual pet name had shaken her.

"Yes. I never called anyone that before you. But there's still so much I want to learn about you."

"But Michael, whatever you felt, whatever you think you still feel, it's just some chemical reaction.

We haven't known each other long enough for it to be anything more. And the baby doesn't change that."

"But maybe some time will," he said. "Time to get to know each other, to let whatever this is grow."

"So what do you suggest?"

"Conversation and dinner. You're looking far too pale for my liking. I don't want you passing out like you did at the airport. So we eat and we let all our worries about the future go for now. Let's just talk, and learn more about each other."

"But—"

"Ah, ah, ah," he scolded. "Let it go, Cara. You've been working yourself crazy with wedding plans, and you've obviously been worrying over our situation."

"*My* situation."

"Stubborn." He shook his head. "I never would have thought you'd be so stubborn."

"See, it just goes to show how little you know me."

"Shh. Eat. The chef has outdone herself."

Michael watched as Cara picked at dinner as they talked, sharing childhood stories. She was pushing things around on her plate more than really eating.

It was driving him mad. Didn't she know she needed to eat properly for her sake and their baby's? There had been pages and pages online about nutrition during pregnancy. Things their baby needed to be healthy.

Folic acid.

Plenty of protein and calcium.

All the recommendations plagued Michael as he watched Cara not eating. Their baby needed that food.

Their baby.

The words sounded sweet in his head, but he kept them to himself. For the time being.

He'd remembered a sweetness about Cara. A gentleness that had robbed him of common sense. But he was discovering a certain hardness under that. She wasn't a woman who was going to be pushed into anything.

And as much as it was frustrating his plans, he respected it.

It was going to take time and effort to show her that they belonged together. But in the end she'd see.

She had to see, because he couldn't lose her again.

"You got quiet," she said, as she played with the asparagus on her plate.

"Just thinking."

"Something tells me that's dangerous." She offered him a quick smile. "So what were you thinking about? Or do I not want to know?"

"I was wondering if the food isn't to your liking. You've spent more time moving things from one side of the plate to the other than eating."

"I'm sorry. I don't want to be rude, but the sauce is a little rich and I've had problems with heartburn—" She clamped a hand over her mouth and looked decidedly embarrassed.

"What's wrong?"

"I don't think discussing my stomach upset is the kind of dinner conversation a prince is used to." Her cheeks were a bright pink.

"It is when it's the mother of his child he's conversing with. It's a pregnancy thing. I read about that this afternoon. You're entering your second trimester and the morning sickness and fatigue should get better, but you'll start having more breast tenderness and—"

"I think you can stop right there," Cara said.

She was blushing furiously.

Michael found it endearing. "Fine. But I also know our baby is about an inch long and has its organs by now. It's such a miracle, Cara."

She didn't bring up her ridiculous Stuart. She simply nodded and said, "It is."

"But you still need to eat sensibly. So, if you'll finish your vegetables, I think I have just the thing for dessert."

"You're bribing me like some child?"

"I'm urging you for the sake of our child."

She ate the last of the asparagus. "There."

He got up and moved to a cooling unit the staff had provided. "Homemade ice cream. The chef claims all Americans have a love affair with the sweet. And you're supposed to be getting plenty of calcium, so it's actually good for you."

"I like how you think." She studied the glass bowl. "What kind is it?"

"Some chocolate-cheesecake concoction she swears will leave you swooning at my feet."

"I think your chef overestimates my love of ice cream. There's no way I can eat all this."

"Try it," Michael commanded.

With agonizing slowness, Cara raised the spoon to her mouth, slid it in and savored the taste.

"Oh, my," she whispered after she'd swallowed.

"Told you," Michael couldn't help but point out.

"I don't know if I'm exactly swooning." She was grinning, teasing him.

Michael loved seeing her like this, and kept his tone light, hoping to maintain the growing ease. "It was close. And by the end of the bowl I have no doubt you will be."

She laughed. "You definitely have a healthy-sized ego."

"It's not ego, it's simply having watched you savor that first bite, I have to acknowledge the chef was right."

Cara was still smiling as she took the next bite, then the next. Michael took a few bites himself, and though he thought it was as good as anything the chef made, he obviously wasn't as in love with the frozen confection as Cara was.

"Are you going to finish that?" Cara asked, eyeing what was left of his dessert.

"No."

"Good." She slid the bowl across the table and took a bite.

Her reaction to the ice cream was going to feature prominently in his dreams tonight.

"You do know that's going to cost you?" he asked, his voice sounding hoarse to his own ears.

NOVEL ™

An Important Message from the Editors

Dear Reader,

you'd enjoy reading novels about rediscovery and reconnection with what's important in women's lives, then let us send you two free Harlequin® Next™ novels. These books celebrate the "next" stage of a woman's life because there's a whole new world after marriage and motherhood.

By the way, you'll also get a surprise gift with your two free books! Please enjoy the free books and gift with our compliments...

Pam Powers

off Seal and

Place Inside...

FREE GIFT
SEAL
EDITOR'S
THANK YOU

THE EDITOR'S "THANK YOU" FREE GIFTS INCLUDE:

▶ Two BRAND-NEW Harlequin® Next™ Novels

▶ An exciting surprise gift

YES! I have placed my Editor's "thank you" Free Gifts seal in the space provided at right. Please send me 2 FREE books, and my FREE Mystery Gift. I understand that I am under no obligation to purchase anything further, as explained on the back and opposite page.

PLACE FREE GIFTS SEAL HERE

356 HDL D72K   156 HDL D73J

FIRST NAME	LAST NAME

ADDRESS

APT.#	CITY

STATE/PROV.	ZIP/POSTAL CODE

Thank You!

(HN-TL-11/05)

The Reader Service — Here's How It Works:

Accepting your 2 free books and gift places you under no obligation to buy anything. You may keep the books and gift and return the shipping statement marked "cancel." If you do not cancel, about a month later we'll send you 3 additional books and bill you just $3.99 each in the U.S., or $4.74 each in Canada, plus 25¢ shipping & handling per book and applicable taxes if any.* That's the complete price and — compared to cover prices of $5.50 each in the U.S. and $6.50 each in Canada — it's quite a bargain! You may cancel at any time, but if you choose to continue, every month we'll send you 3 more books, which you may either purchase at the discount price or return to us and cancel your subscription.

*Terms and prices subject to change without notice. Sales tax applicable in N.Y. Canadian residents will be charged applicable provincial taxes and GST.

"What's the going price for a half-eaten, rapidly melting bowl of ice cream?"

"A kiss."

She pushed the bowl back into the middle of the table. "No way."

"Sorry. You've already eaten some of it, so you owe me the going price. I don't think you're the type of woman who doesn't pay her debts."

"There's no debt. You didn't tell me there was a price. That's not fair."

He laughed. "Every one knows the going rate for ice cream."

"You weren't eating it," she protested. "If I hadn't helped you out, it would have gone to waste and your chef might have been insulted."

"Is kissing me such a hardship?" he asked softly.

She sighed and didn't look at all happy as she admitted, "You know it's not. And that's the problem when you get down to it. Kissing you isn't a problem at all, and it should be. It should be a big problem."

"Just a little kiss. Nothing big at all."

She hesitated another moment, and Michael was sure she was going to say no again, but she didn't say anything. She merely leaned across the table and planted a light kiss on his lips, then immediately pulled back.

"There. We're even," she said.

"I don't think you can call that much of a kiss." He shook his head. "I'm not even sure if it could be called a peck."

"Ah, but I didn't eat much of your ice cream, so even by your warped logic it didn't require much of a kiss for repayment."

"Are you going to eat the rest?" he asked, hopefully.

Cara couldn't help it, she laughed. "Ha. You wish. You can't catch me like that again."

"Coward."

"No. Just too smart for the likes of you." She rose. "And now, if you don't mind, I think it's time that I left."

He rose and followed her to the door. "Good night, *cara mia.*"

"We didn't solve anything," she said.

"We can't solve anything until you're willing to agree to marry me."

"Michael, it could never work."

Maybe it was just wishful thinking, but Michael thought he heard a bit of wistfulness in her voice.

"I won't stop asking you," he assured her. "I can't."

"And I can't give you the answer you're looking for. So where does that leave us?"

"A stalemate."

She turned and left. Michael simply stood there watching her.

Yes, they'd reached a stalemate, but eventually she would see the sense in his proposal.

Soon she'd say yes.

He was sure of it.

Well, almost sure.

Six

The next morning Cara awoke with a groan, and immediately sank back into her pillow. Her stomach wasn't fond of mornings.

Maybe she should nickname this baby *Lurch*. That's what her stomach had done every day for the last few weeks.

She had taken to leaving crackers on the nightstand and eating one before even trying to get up. Last night she'd forgotten to leave them out.

It was all Michael's fault.

Michael and his wild, crazy, off-the-wall, it-could-never-work-in-this-lifetime-or-any-other idea.

Marry him?

Right.

He was a prince and she was a part owner of a bookstore.

Of course, a little voice in her head whispered, Parker was a princess and was marrying a P.I., and Shey was part owner of a coffeehouse and was marrying a prince.

That wasn't it at all.

Her hand moved instinctually to her stomach. It wasn't what he was and what she was. It was who they were.

Strangers.

He didn't love her. He desired her, that much was true. And she desired him.

But love?

No. They hardly knew each other.

They were having a baby together, but he didn't know anything meaningful about her, or her about him.

He didn't love her.

That was the sticking point.

He didn't love her and Cara wasn't settling for anything less than what Parker and Shey had found.

There was a knock on her bedroom door.

She moved gingerly into a sitting position, worried that her stomach might rebel, but thankfully it gave a token protest, then settled back down.

She got all the way up, tossed on a robe and went to the door.

"Who is it?" she said, suddenly very aware that she was still in her pajamas.

"Dr. Stevens. Tom."

She hid behind the door and opened it a crack.

"Good morning," she said, smiling.

"Are you all right?" he asked, concern in his voice.

"I'm fine." At his questioning look, she assured him, "Absolutely fine. And you?"

He ignored her question and studied her. "I was worried and decided to come check up on you."

"Why would you be worried?"

Did she look that bad? After all, she'd been a bit nauseous, but she didn't think she could look that green because of it. Her stomach was actually settling down quite nicely. She remembered what Michael had said about morning sickness getting better after the third month.

He'd been reading about pregnancy. Though she shouldn't let it, the thought warmed her.

"I was worried because we had an appointment this morning. You were going to meet me in the garden, remember?"

"We weren't supposed to meet until eleven." She glanced at her wrist to see what time it was, but she hadn't put her watch on yet.

Tommy saw the gesture and said, "Cara, it's noon." He glanced at his own wristwatch. "Ten after if you'd like to be exact."

No way was it that late.

She looked back toward her nightstand, but it was too far away for her to see the small clock. "Really, it couldn't be. I never sleep in, and I never, ever miss an appointment."

"Today it appears you've done both," he said with a quick grin. "But if you agree to meet me in the dining room as soon as you're dressed I could probably be convinced to forgive you."

Noon? She'd slept in that late? She'd stood up Tommy?

"I'm so embarrassed. I'm so sorry. Yes, I'll meet you in the dining room as quickly as I can."

"Hey, really, it's no problem. You need your sleep. And don't rush. I'll order lunch for us. Brunch in your case," he teased.

Cara allowed herself an answering grin. "I'll be down in just a few minutes."

Cara rushed her dressing, not that she normally spent a long time getting ready. By the time she got to the small dining room the family used for day-to-day meals, Tommy already had a plate in front of him and one across from him.

"Because it's your brunch, I thought a nice fruit salad might be just the thing to start with."

"Perfect," Cara said, indeed feeling as if she could eat the fruit. She took a small bite to see how it would settle.

"The prince called me last night," Tommy said after she'd eaten a few bites.

"He did?" Her stomach did a little flip-flop.

"He wanted to know when pregnant women normally notice the baby moving."

"Oh?" she said, trying to sound nonchalant, but all the while feeling anything but.

"I hesitated and he said he wasn't asking about

anyone specific, just general health knowledge that he had already looked up on the Internet. He just wanted verification."

"What did you tell him?" That small bite of fruit was settling in the bottom of her stomach as heavily as a piece of lead.

"The truth. Women generally feel the first fluttering at the beginning of the second trimester, give or take."

"Oh." The prince wasn't a dunce. If he had any doubts before they'd just been set to rest. He knew that the baby was his.

"I had the fact fairly handy since I've been brushing up on my obstetric lessons lately."

"That's kind of you."

Michael knew. He'd said he'd known before, but he had to be positive now. What was he going to do next?

"He did ask if it was likely that a woman would feel movements in her first or second month. I said no. Then he asked about in her third and I said, yes, more likely in her late third or early fourth."

"Oh," she said again.

"I'm not asking any questions, mind you," Tommy assured her. "But I do want you to know I take patient confidence seriously. The prince was right though, and it was information that could easily be found anywhere."

"It's fine, Tommy," Cara assured him.

"You do know that if you need to talk I'm here. It doesn't have to be strictly medical. I would never betray your trust, or ask questions." He reached across the table and patted her hand in a big-brotherly way.

Cara flipped her hand so she could grip his and give it a quick squeeze. "I'll remember that. I don't know how to thank you for being such a good friend the last couple weeks."

He gave her hand one more squeeze and started, "It's been my pleasure. I just hope—"

Whatever Tommy hoped was going to remain a mystery because a voice interrupted him by saying, "Well, isn't this cozy?"

Not just a voice.

Michael's voice.

Cara jumped, feeling decidedly like a child with her hand caught in the cookie jar. And because she felt guilty, even though she had no call to feel guilty, she glared at Michael.

"Mind if I join you?" Michael asked.

"Feel free," Tommy, the let-me-be-your-big-brother traitor said. He didn't look the least bit caught off guard at Michael's sudden appearance.

"How are you this morning, Cara?" Michael asked, genuine concern in his voice.

"Just fine, thank you, Your Highness," she replied, keeping things as formal as she could manage.

He didn't press any further, but simply nodded. "So what was the topic of conversation this morning? It looked serious."

"Not so much," she assured him. "Just two people who enjoy each other's company sharing a meal."

"Is that so? This doesn't have anything to do with the fainting incident and test results?"

Cara wasn't about to tell him that her test results had been in for a while and that they gave her a clean bill of health. "Even if we were talking about my health, Your Highness, I'm sure you'd agree that my medical care is my concern."

"And mine, as your doctor," Tommy added.

She shot him a look of gratitude and continued, "I've been assured that the details of a person's health are completely confidential."

"Is that a tactful way of telling me to mind my own business?" he asked.

"I'm pretty sure that's just what it is," Cara assured him with a smile that felt brittle.

She pushed back the half-eaten plate of fruit. "Now, if you'll excuse me, gentlemen. I got a late start today and have a bunch of things that need to be attended to, ASAP."

"But you haven't finished your meal," Michael said even as the doctor said, "You need to eat."

"I'm a big girl and have managed my dietary needs for years without help from either of you." Without waiting for anymore of Michael's protesting, she gave Tommy a quick wave and hurried out of the room.

She glanced back over her shoulder and saw Michael talking fast and furiously at Tommy.

Maybe leaving wasn't so wise.

But no, she was sure Tommy would honor her privacy. It was fine.

* * *

"That's not good enough," Michael said, his nerves frayed.

"I'm afraid it's the best I can do," Tom said. "What good would I be as a physician if I didn't honor my patient's wishes?"

"It's my baby," Michael insisted. "I have rights."

"I'm afraid that right now, you don't." Tom Stevens looked sympathetic as he continued. "I truly wish I could tell you something to set your mind at ease, but all I can say is she's my patient and I'm doing my best for her, just as I've always done my best for you."

Michael got up and stalked out of the room.

He'd always liked Tom Stevens and respected the way he did his job. But at this moment, he wished the man wasn't quite such a stickler for ethics.

Michael needed someone on his side. He thought about calling Parker and explaining the situation, but couldn't do it. He might get his sister to plead his case, but he was pretty sure Cara wouldn't appreciate it.

If their roles were reversed, he knew he wouldn't.

No, somehow the two of them were going to have to work things out on their own.

Of course, it would be easier if his sweet *cara mia* hadn't turned out to be a stubborn, aggravating…woman.

But men had wooed women for centuries and had won them over.

Somehow Michael would manage it as well.

* * *

Cara couldn't decipher the odd looks Michael kept shooting her way throughout the very long, formal dinner.

Thankfully she had been seated next to Ambassador McClinnon. He kept her thoroughly entertained throughout the innumerable courses. Actually, it would have been a very enjoyable evening if it weren't for Michael's strange expressions.

What was he up to?

"…And then Pearly said, 'I'm sorry Mrs. Sherbrooke, but y'all never had my mama's pie.'"

She laughed, despite herself.

The ambassador had the same gift of blarney that Pearly Gates had. Maybe it was a regional trait? Or maybe it was just proof that despite the years that separated them, the ambassador and Pearly belonged together.

"She sounds like a riot," Cara said, not letting on that she knew his Pearly.

She'd talked to Parker and Shey, and they'd all agreed that it should be a surprise. Pearly would be here in Eliason soon for the wedding.

And so would the ambassador. Pearly's Buster.

Cara couldn't wait. She felt like a matchmaker.

"A riot," the ambassador assured her. "That was my Pearly. She had a way of lighting up a room, and always seemed to know just what to say. I don't know why she's been on my mind so much lately."

He drifted, and Cara could almost see him make the journey back in time. "One of the last times I saw

Pearly was at a reception for a friend. I'd brought a date, really just a friend. But I could have kicked myself, because try as I might, Pearly made it pretty clear she was avoiding me. But I came up behind her as she was talking to Francie Dryer. Francie was lamenting the fact that she wasn't expecting yet, and she'd been married all of a year. Pearly looked at her and said, 'Mama always said, babies come in their own time. Maybe God's just taking his time and looking for the right baby for you.'"

"And Francie felt better?" Cara asked.

"At the time I think she did. But it turned out Francie's *right* baby was a bit of a rascal, and over the next few years she had four more. All boys. And according to the town gossips, all more than slightly prone to trouble."

"I'm sure they were worth the trouble." Cara caught herself before her hand slipped to her own stomach, and instead folded her hands on her lap.

Lurch was already giving her a bit of trouble, but she was sure she could handle it.

Just as she was sure this baby was her right baby. She hoped it would have Michael's dark hair rather than her mousy brown.

Maybe her baby would have Michael's blue eyes. But how would she feel year after year, looking at a tangible reminder of the man she couldn't have?

Trouble. Yes, that pretty much described her situation. Between a rock and a hard place. And if the gleam in Michael's eye was an indication, her hard place was about to get a bit harder.

"Yes, I think Francie would agree that they were worth the trouble." He paused, looking wistful. "Maybe after these weddings, I'll make a trip home."

"And look for Pearly?"

"I didn't say that," he said quickly, too quickly.

"I don't think you had to."

"Knowing Pearly, she remembers exactly what our last fight was about and still bears a grudge."

"Maybe. Maybe not. Wouldn't it be fun to find out?" Cara asked.

The ambassador smiled. "Yes. Yes, I think it would be."

Cara felt like a child at Christmas, knowing a big secret she couldn't share with anyone. She couldn't wait until the Perry Square contingent started arriving. Pearly and the ambassador would be in for a surprise.

"Babies," Michael said from across the table. "I couldn't help but hear your story, Ambassador. They can be trouble. But of course, I wasn't, was I, Mother?

All Cara's glee evaporated and she turned, feeling sick to her stomach. Michael wouldn't.

He couldn't.

"You?" his mother said, smiling at the end of the table. "I agree with your Pearly, even the most troublesome rascals are worth it—"

"Mother, are you saying I was a troublesome rascal?" Michael blustered, even as he grinned.

"I didn't say it," the queen assured him. "You did. But I'm not arguing. I can't wait until Parker and her

Jace are married. I want to be a grandmother. I'll spoil my grandchildren rotten."

Cara couldn't help it, she choked.

The ambassador reached for her glass of water and handed it to her. She managed a sip and tried to ignore the rush of heat to her cheeks.

"Are you all right?" Michael asked, the picture of innocence.

Cara sent him an evil look, which made Michael's smile even bigger.

"I'm fine," she assured the rat.

He nodded and turned back to the queen. "I hope that I can help fulfill your wish someday soon, Mother."

"Have you found someone?" his mother asked. "That lovely reporter who visited? Is there something you'd like to share with us?"

"Not quite yet, but soon. There will hopefully be news for you soon."

"It's so cruel to tease me," his mother chastised, but he could see she was pleased with his comments. "Won't you just give me a hint?"

"Maybe just a little one," he said.

"No," Cara said. All eyes turned to her. "I mean, if the prince isn't sure enough about the relationship to share it, we should allow him his privacy. I know that I wouldn't want anyone to analyze my life."

"I think Cara has a point," Michael said. "Things are so new in this relationship that I want to take some time to figure things out before I share the details."

"But—" the queen started.

"Darling, I think it would be best if we give our son the time he's requested," the king said.

"That's not what you said when it was Parker's life you were meddling in," his wife pointed out.

"That was different," he blustered. "I wasn't meddling in her love life, I just wanted her to come home."

"And you've got your wish," a new voice said.

Parker and Jace walked into the room.

"Parker," Michael cried.

"Parker," Cara said. "You're early."

"I decided that I wanted time for Mom and Dad to get to know Jace better before the wedding."

Her parents jumped up and pretty soon they were all entangled in a hug. A family, reunited.

Cara wondered if they would all greet her baby like that when it came to visit them. She watched the king and queen as they held Parker and saw how much they missed her. Would it be the same for Michael? Would the time spent apart from his child be filled with that kind of longing?

Parker made her way around the table and hugged Cara. "You look different," she said, staring at her assessingly.

Cara didn't know how to answer, so she simply asked, "Where's Shey?"

"She and Tanner are with his parents. They'll be here next week."

Extra place settings were brought out. Parker sat next to Cara, Jace across from her, next to Michael. The two men were quickly carrying on a quiet conversation.

"Are you okay?" Parker asked quietly as she slid into the hastily prepared seat next to Cara.

Cara glared at Michael, knowing full well why Parker was asking the question—why Parker had come home early.

She turned to Parker and gave her a quick hug as she answered, "Yes, of course, I'm fine. Why wouldn't I be?"

"I…well…" Parker glanced at Michael and Cara knew he'd been talking to her.

"Whatever tales the prince has been telling are highly exaggerated. I'm absolutely fine."

Parker didn't look convinced. "We'll talk later."

"We can talk about the wedding, talk about how wonderful Jace is. There's a lot to talk about. But we don't need to talk about me because I'm absolutely fine."

"Parker," the queen said, "tell me more about the store."

"Well…" Parker launched with enthusiasm into tales of her misadventures as a coffee shop and bookstore owner. But now and again she glanced purposely at Cara.

Cara couldn't wait for the long meal to end. As soon as politeness would allow, she excused herself.

"Can we talk?" Parker asked as she rose.

"Maybe tomorrow. You need to catch up with your parents. I'm exhausted and just want to get some sleep."

It was probably the wrong thing to say because

she could see the concern on Parker's face. But she ignored it as she hugged her friend good-night and left the formal dining room.

The pig.

The royal, can't-fight-his-own-battles, call-in-re-inforcements jerk.

"Cara, wait," his High-and-Jerkiness hollered as she hurried down the hall toward her room.

Cara didn't slow her pace one iota. As a matter of fact, she walked even faster.

"Cara."

And faster yet.

She was practically jogging, but she didn't care, she just couldn't face Michael right now. She, who rarely felt the least bit of ire, was fuming. If he forced a confrontation now she was bound to say something she'd regret.

"Cara." He grabbed her by the shoulder and spun her around. "I didn't call her."

"Liar."

"Okay, I did call her, but just for reassurance. I didn't ask her to come home early, even though I thought about it. It would be nice to have someone on my side, someone to lend moral support."

"Moral support? Reassurance? What kind of reassurance could she give you?"

"Hearing her talk about Jace, and the happiness she'd found with him makes me believe we can find that as well."

Cara didn't say anything because she didn't know what to say.

"I was as surprised as you when she walked into the dining room," he said gently.

"Liar. You hoped your call would bring her home."

"Cara, honey, you can call me all kinds of names, but I've never lied to you. I never will. Which is why when I say I want to marry you, or when I say I didn't call Parker home, you can believe me."

She felt herself begin to relax a little. "Really?"

"Really," he assured her. "I meant it when I said I never have and I never will lie to you."

"Well, thanks. If you didn't call her home, then why is she here early?"

"I imagine she's here to see Mom and Dad, just like she said. I understand that the days before a wedding are jittery ones."

"Oh."

"Cara, you know when I said I wouldn't lie to you?"

"Yes."

"You believe me, right?"

She would have liked to say no, but she saw the vulnerability in his eyes and said, "Yes, I guess so."

Vulnerability and something else.

"So then when I tell you that I want to kiss you right now—kiss you until you can't see straight, until your knees give way, until you can't breathe, you'd believe me?"

Her throat felt dry. She knew she should tell him no, that kissing him was the last thing she wanted, but she couldn't lie. She settled for saying, "You could tell me that, but that doesn't mean I'd agree to it."

"Ah, but I didn't hear you disagree."

"I—"

"You want me as much as I want you." Before she could respond, he added, "No lying."

"What makes you think you need to warn me? You think I'd lie?"

"Professor Stuart," he said simply.

"That's different. We've been through this. If there's a Stuart, you're off the hook."

"I don't want to be off the hook, I want to—" He didn't finish the sentence with words. Instead, he demonstrated just what he wanted.

Cara was done denying that she wanted him as much as he claimed to want her.

Every time she touched him, every time he touched her, all her worries and doubts flew out the window and all that was left was the certainty that this man was the one she'd been waiting for.

She relaxed in his arms, wrapping herself in Michael. Her lips melded to his, instant with desire.

"Eh hem," someone behind Michael said.

Cara recognized the throat clearing.

She pulled away and peeked behind him. "Parker, I can explain."

"I'm sure you can, and I can't wait to hear that explanation." She turned to Michael. "Big brother, do you mind if I borrow my friend for a moment?"

"I do, but I'll let you. Consider my sharing Cara a wedding gift."

"You're just too cheap to buy me something nice," Parker said.

"I'd say Cara qualifies as something more than nice."

"I'd be forced to agree, and because I recognize her value, I'd be remiss as a friend if I didn't warn you that if you hurt her…" She left the threat hanging.

Cara knew she should feel warmed by the thought that Parker cared enough to threaten her brother, but instead she felt annoyed. "Parker, I'm right here, and I'm pretty sure I'm capable of taking care of myself."

Parker ignored her and kept her attention on Michael, who said, "And I guess I should be just as up front with you, little sister, when I tell you I've asked Cara to marry me."

"What?" Parker said, obviously taken aback.

"I said no," Cara hastily assured her.

"You practically just met. You hardly know each other." Parker eyed them both.

"About that—" Michael started.

"Not another word from either of you," Cara said. "I'm quite capable of protecting myself, just as I'm quite capable of deciding who I'll marry. Fact is, I turned your brother down, Parker."

This time it was Cara on the receiving end of Parker's glare. "Why would you turn him down? He might be a pain as a brother, but rumor has it that women who aren't his sister find him a catch."

"They're welcome to catch him all they want. I'm not interested."

"From what I just witnessed, I'd have to say, you looked more than interested."

"Ah, you see," Michael said, "your friend is a fickle woman. She likes kissing me well enough, but her heart belongs to Professor Stuart. She's going to run home to the jerk."

"Stuart who?" Parker asked.

Cara didn't answer her. She was too busy glaring at Michael, the tattletaling, I-won't-lie-to-you snitch. "Stuart's a good man, I told you that."

"You told me many things, *cara mia.*" His voice had that soft little burr to it that got to her.

"Don't call me that."

"Cara mia," he said again, taunting her, then he leaned down and kissed her forehead. "I'll leave you with my sister to talk. I'll go find my future brother-in-law."

"You do that," Parker said. She turned toward Cara, a thousand questions in her eyes as she continued, "Sounds like there's a lot that's gone on here in the last couple weeks. Maybe it's about time you bring me up to speed."

Seven

The minute Michael was out of sight, Parker dragged Cara to a sitting room she'd never seen before. That was no surprise. She was sure there were many rooms she still hadn't visited.

This was one of the homier rooms. An inviting sitting area, a huge fireplace.

"So?" Parker said as soon as they'd settled on a sofa.

Cara felt uncomfortable under Parker's intense scrutiny. "Stop staring at me like that."

Her hand started to drift to her stomach, as if by covering it, she could hide the fact it was rounding more than slightly, but she caught herself and kept both hands firmly planted on her lap.

"Spill it," Parker said, no request in the two words. It was a rather regal order.

"You're pretty much caught up. What more is there to tell? Your brother asked me to marry him, I said no."

Parker scoffed. "There's more—a lot more—to this story. And if you don't tell me, I'm calling in Shey. You know she'll have you talking in minutes."

Cara could picture Shey's withering glare and knew that Parker was right, she'd crack.

Not ready to bow to the inevitable, she tried a delaying tactic. "Fine. I'll tell you everything, but I'd rather wait until after the wedding. Then we'll all have a heart-to-heart. You, me and Shey. The three of us."

Parker shook her head with such ferocity that her blond hair whipped back and forth. "Sorry, no can do. This is big and I suspect you need me, even if you don't want to admit it. Let me be here for you."

Cara felt her eyes fill with tears again. She wasn't a crier, had never been a crier, and suddenly it seemed she was always on the edge of tears. She blinked hard a couple times, hoping to hold them at bay, then said, "Parker, this is your time. I want you to focus on Jace. An intimate, romantic ceremony… Then in another month, a huge full-blown one for the public. Two weddings to the same man. It's every woman's dream. Concentrate on that. I'm fine."

Her heart gave a small tug at the thought that she'd never have the kind of love Jace and Parker shared.

She and Michael did have something together. *Chemistry* would probably be the best word to describe it. But she wanted more. She wanted what Parker and Shey had found.

"Cara, honey," Parker took her hand and gave it a squeeze. "I love Jace, and there's no need to concentrate on it. It just is. It's my constant. Loving him is sort of the center of everything for me. So, there's no need to wait to tell me. I can see something big is going on and I want to be here for you. Please don't shut me out."

Cara had known that keeping things from Parker was a losing battle, even if she'd felt the need to try.

"Okay," she said, admitting defeat. "It's more than just your brother asking me to marry him. The thing is…"

The sentence trailed off as Cara tried to decide how to say what needed to be said. She knew there was no way to soften the shock, so she just blurted out, "I'm pregnant. Your brother was just being noble—doing the *right* thing. I did say no because I deserve more than that. So does he. We both deserved more than someone trying to do the right thing."

Parker didn't say anything, though her shock was evident in her expression.

"I can't marry your brother," Cara continued hastily. "And I can see the worries starting, so let me assure you that I have it all planned. The baby can come to Titles with me. I know you and Shey won't mind, not that Shey will be there, she'll be with Tanner. But now that we've hired Shelly, she can take over while I'm on maternity leave, and help when I come back. How are things with her and Peter going? Are they still hot and heavy?"

"No changing the subject," Parker scolded. "I'm still adjusting my reality to the fact you're going to be a mother. Who's this professor that Michael was talking about? And why isn't he asking to marry you?"

Part of Cara wanted to keep the myth of Professor Stuart alive. It would be so much easier. And although she was pretty sure she could keep the professor story going with most of the world, she couldn't lie to her friends.

"There is no professor," she said softly. "I made him up. Michael's the father."

"Michael? But how? It's only been—"

"A little over three months," Cara supplied.

"Three months?" Parker repeated.

Cara saw the dawn of understanding on Parker's face. "When he came on his last-ditch mission to bring me home?"

Cara nodded. "I didn't know who he was. He didn't know who I was. We met and it was an instant connection. I've never experienced anything like it."

And she was sure it would never happen again. Lightning didn't strike the same place twice.

"You're the mystery woman he's had Jace searching for?" Parker murmured.

She shrugged. "He did say he'd been looking."

She hadn't quite decided how to handle that information. Hadn't figured out just what it meant.

"And this is his baby?" Parker asked. Then the realization sank in and she grinned. "Oh my, this *is* my brother's baby, which means it's my niece or nephew. I'm going to be an aunt."

"No one can know that except you and Shey. No one else. As far as everyone else is concerned, Professor Stuart is the father."

Parker's happy smile faded. "But why?"

"You of all people need to ask me that? If your brother is the baby's father, that means the baby is royal, and with that comes all the baggage you're so anxious to get rid of. And can you imagine what the reporters would make of a prince's illegitimate child? What kind of life would the baby have? Do you want that for your niece or nephew? Being hounded by the media? Look at the lengths you've gone to in order to have a small, private wedding ceremony before the more public affair."

"Cara, I may not want this life, but I had a choice. How can you take that choice away from the baby? How can you deny your child his or her heritage?" She took a deep breath and looked as if she were trying to calm herself before she continued. "How can you deny Michael the right to be the father I know he will be?"

"I don't know, Parker. That's the truth of it. It's all happening so fast. I didn't know who Michael was until the airport. The only pictures I ever saw of him were taken when you were both small. I don't know what to do. I need time to figure out what's right for all three of us. I need to keep Professor Stu around for at least a while."

Parker didn't look happy about it, but slowly she nodded. "For a while. But Cara, the professor won't work long-term."

"I know. I—" She stopped short. "Can we just talk about something else for a while? Anything. Let's talk about Pearly and Buster."

Parker reached across the couch and squeezed her shoulder. "Yeah, we can. And when you're ready, I'll be here. Let me be here for you."

Cara nodded. Tears were pooling in her eyes as the emotion clogged her throat. She couldn't push any words out past it all, so she simply leaned over and hugged Parker.

When she let go, Parker said, "Now, about the Pearly situation. I asked her to come early. She'll be here in a few days. You haven't said anything to the ambassador?"

"Not a word. Watching them meet again after all this time…" Cara sighed and felt a wave of wistfulness sweep through her.

Having heard both Pearly and the ambassador talk of the other, she was sure this meeting would be special. It would be romantic.

And right now, Cara needed a romance to work out for someone.

Michael didn't know what to do with himself as he waited for Cara and Parker to break up their little talk. Pacing the hall wasn't much of a solution, but it was the best he could come up with. Pacing and wondering what his sister was saying to Cara.

Maybe Cara would confide in Parker. Maybe Parker would convince Cara to give him a chance.

Maybe.

The *maybes* were killing him.

Why couldn't Cara see that they were meant to be together? What would it take to prove to her that he'd do anything for her and their child?

"Thinking about her?" Jace O'Donnell, the man who would be marrying his sister in a very short time, asked as he rounded the corner and entered Michael's pacing zone.

He knew Cara didn't want their relationship divulged, so he simply said, "Yes. I can't seem to stop thinking of her."

"Tell me about it. Once I met Parker I couldn't get her out of my head or my heart. And man, that sounds lame even to me, but there it is."

"You tried?" Michael asked, surprised. His sister was…well, he'd never admit it to her, but she was an amazing woman. "You tried to get over your feelings for Parker?"

"Repeatedly," Jace assured him.

"But why?"

Jace gave him a look that sort of said, *Duh*.

Michael shook his head and shrugged his shoulders. *Duh* or no *duh*, he didn't get it.

"She's a princess, I'm a P.I.," Jace finally said. "She's royalty, and I'm…well, I'm not. It took me a while to see that our worlds could fit. That our differences made us stronger."

"When she talks about you anyone can see that it

doesn't matter." Michael shook his head. "I went to Erie to convince her to come home, but it only took a few minutes to realize she'd never come home except on visits. She'd met you and that was it."

That's how it had been when he'd met Cara. It. No going back. No turning around.

Cara was simply *it* for him.

"It was fast," Jace admitted. "That's part of what took me by surprise, the speed."

"That's how it goes in my family. Fast. You meet the right person and it's…"

"Lightning," Jace supplied.

"Yes, lightning," Michael agreed. "Immediate. It's just there. You can't miss it."

Well, he couldn't miss it, but obviously Cara could.

"I'm sorry I was never able to find your mystery woman for you." Jace slapped his shoulder in a brotherly show of sympathy.

"That's all right." Michael would have liked to have told Jace, but he was sure Cara wouldn't appreciate it. Look at how she'd reacted when she'd thought he'd called Parker home.

"I know we don't know each other well yet," Jace said. "But if you want to talk about it, I'm here."

"Thanks. I appreciate that, appreciate all you've done." Michael liked this man his sister was going to marry. There was something very genuine about him.

"Nothing to appreciate. You're family."

Family.

That was important.

Why couldn't Cara see that they were meant to be a family, that she was meant to be with him?

Somehow he was going to convince her that they were meant to be together.

Jace had said it had taken him a while to see that his world and Parker's worked together.

Cara had experienced just a small taste of Eliason, of his world. Maybe he'd give her a little more. Show her that she could contribute and enjoy aspects of the life he offered her.

Show her that their worlds meshed.

That they should be a family.

"Would you come with me today?" he asked the next day when he cornered Cara eating a hurried breakfast. "Just a short outing. No questions, no arguments, no Professor Stu."

"Why?"

"Just because I asked. Because at dinner the other night, we mentioned trying to get to know more about one another. I'd like a chance to let you see a bit of what I do."

"No talk of marriage or babies?" she countered.

"Cross my heart."

He was up to something. She could sense it, but for the life of her, she couldn't figure out what.

She should say no. She needed to keep her distance, maintain some perspective. But he looked so excited, and that enthusiasm was contagious because she found herself saying, "I can't be gone too long. I have work to do. The wedding's just around the corner."

"Now that Parker's here, some of the pressure on you should be lifted." He was leading her toward the main entryway.

"Just where are we going?"

"A quick trip to St. Mark's. A surprise."

He settled her in the limo and kept up a steady stream of chatter about the capital, pointing out various sights, filling her in on local history until the car came to a stop in front of an impressive brick building.

"St. Mark's main library," Michael told her before she could even ask. "They have a story time once a week, and today I'm the guest reader. I thought it might be something you'd enjoy."

Cara didn't know what to say, so she simply allowed Michael to lead her through the grand building into a small, cozy children's area. That he'd thought about this, about something that would please her, touched her.

She noted that some of Michael's bodyguards were discreetly spread throughout the area, but he didn't seem to pay any attention to them. His focus was completely on the group of preschool children.

After a quick introduction by the librarian, he settled in and began reading a short picture book.

Watching him, listening to him do the voices and make sound effects, she could almost picture him holding their child and doing the same. The mental image tugged at her heart. She got lost in the fantasy, then abruptly realized he'd finished.

"I was wondering if you would like another story?" he asked the group. "I brought along my friend, Cara. She's from America. And rumor has it, she does a lot of story times at her bookstore." He looked at her. "Cara?"

There was nothing for her to do but move to the front of the room. Michael handed her a book. She looked down and saw *Little Red Riding Hood* and couldn't help but laugh.

"You planned this," she whispered.

"Guilty," he said.

One of the little boys raised his hand, then immediately blurted out, "Are you the prince's princess?"

Michael watched her, obviously waiting for her answer along with all the children in the room.

She shook her head. "No, I'm just a friend."

"But maybe someday she'll be my princess," Michael assured the boy.

Cara shot him a *behave* look, and ignored the rest of the children whose hands flew into the air and the speculative look on the librarian's face. "If you'll all sit down, I'll start. Once upon a time…"

She fell easily into the rhythm of the story. It was natural to her—reading to a group of children, surrounded by books.

During her time in Eliason, she'd been out of her element entirely. Castles, princes, pregnancy—she hadn't realized how much stress she felt, until she re-entered her comfort zone.

She tried to ignore Michael, who was sitting cross-legged on the floor, a group of children huddled around him. It painted an endearing picture. Like his care for his family, his devotion to his country, his obvious affection for children was something that pulled at her.

If she could just pretend he wasn't here, maybe this brief respite would help her regain some sense of equilibrium. But there was no pretending. Michael seemed to always be at the forefront of her awareness.

"…The end." The children clapped. And at the librarian's suggestion, they began asking questions.

"What books do you like?" a cute blond girl asked.

"Harry Potter?" a boy shouted.

Cara breathed a sigh of relief. Here was a subject she could deal with. "I love Harry Potter, but he wasn't around when I was little. When I was your age, or a little older, I read C. S. Lewis's Narnia books. And Trixie Belden, L'Engle, Cleary…" She kept up a stream of titles and authors.

As she finished, another hand shot up. She nodded at a little redheaded boy. "Do you have any children?"

She caught herself as her hand began to move to her slightly rounded abdomen. "Not yet," she replied honestly.

More hands.

"Are you and the prince going to get married?"

"No, the prince and I are just very good friends." That is if you could call a rat a friend. With no warning at all he'd thrust her into his awkward position.

"Speaking of friends, I have a very good friend who's counting on me, so I really should be going."

On cue, Michael stood and came up to the front of the crowd. Cara watched him as he flawlessly made their excuses and said goodbye. She wasn't sure what today was about.

Why had he invited her along on this public appearance?

He casually steered her through the crowd of children and parents, stopping to chat now and again.

By the time they finally reached the limo, Cara's confusion had her stomach in a knot.

Michael could tell Cara was annoyed. It didn't take a rocket scientist to see that. She'd stewed silently most of the way back to the castle, then abruptly blurted out, "Would you mind telling me what that was all about?"

"Well, you'd mentioned Red Riding Hood, so I knew you were familiar with the story, and I find it's easier to read books out loud that you know, so I—"

"Not the story choice. Why did you bring me along?"

"Because I'm hoping that eventually you'll say yes to my marriage proposal, and I thought it might be a good idea for you to get a feel for what it is I do. Not just reading stories at libraries, but opening hospital wings, and all the other public appearances. It's part of the job. Part of bearing the title. There's a business side, too. There are a lot of facets of being royal."

"But, I'm no princess."

"I'm hoping, someday soon, you will be. And I wanted to show you that our worlds aren't all that different. That we could fit together."

She slipped back into silence, and Michael didn't push any further.

He'd wanted to share with her some of what he did. It might not seem like much, but reading to kids, lending his name to various events, meant something to the people of Eliason, which made it an important aspect of his job.

He wanted her to know, because he'd meant what he'd said—someday soon he hoped she'd be taking a part, too.

With every passing day he became more sure of what he wanted. It was simple really. He wanted Cara and their baby.

What wasn't so simple was convincing Cara. Why couldn't she see that they had a chance at something special. Something his parents had. Something he'd been searching for before he even realized he wanted it.

He knew that if Cara Phillips gave him her heart, it would be forever.

That's all Michael was asking for.

Forever.

Cara got out of the limo and jumped right back into a whirlwind of activity, but throughout the day Michael's words kept intruding.

And I wanted to show you that our worlds aren't all that different. That we could fit together.

Could they?

She pushed the thought away. Thankfully there were still so many arrangements to be made that she didn't have time to think about Michael, about their outing, about what she was going to do.

At least she didn't have much time. But his words occasionally crept in. ...*we could fit together.*

By that night she'd exhausted herself and should have slept like the dead, but the questions kept spinning in her head. Could she do it? Could she stay here in Eliason?

Sleep wouldn't come. She tossed and turned, worrying about what to do. What was the fair solution for herself, for Michael, and most importantly, for their baby?

She got up the next day and did it all again. Frenzied work, restless night, questions chasing themselves round and round in her head.

...our worlds aren't all that different. That we could fit together.

Two mornings later, after the library visit, Cara was at her makeshift desk checking messages, when she noticed a book that hadn't been there when she'd left. She looked at the title. *Nine Months.*

Sections were highlighted.

A pregnancy time line had hurdles checked off, other sections with question marks by them.

Another section was marked. She flipped to it and found a week-by-week photo journal of a baby's development. One had writing next to it. *Our baby this week.*

The tears welling in her eyes began to fall in earnest.

Not just a few tears, but all-out crying. Tiny sobs that she tried to hold in but eventually erupted.

Cara didn't cry prettily. No Hollywood tears here. Her eyes felt raw and her nose was running like a spigot.

Our baby this week.

Michael had obviously spent all his spare time reading the book, trying to understand what she was going through. Why? Because he loved this baby.

She realized she'd known that all along.

He loved their baby as much as she did.

How on earth could she go back to Erie and take their baby with her? Michael couldn't follow. He had responsibilities here.

She cried even harder.

What was she going to do? How could she make this situation work out fairly for both herself and Michael? Even more importantly, how could she make things right for their baby?

Somehow she had to get these darned pregnancy hormones under control. She was tired of crying. Tired of feeling unsure.

"*Cara mia,* what's wrong?" Michael, aka The Shadow, came into the office.

"You have to stop stalking me." She sniffed and brushed at her eyes.

"What's wrong?" he repeated.

"Nothing." She slid the book under a pile of papers.

He spotted it and pulled it out. "You found the book."

"It wasn't fair."

"It wasn't meant to be," he assured softly.

Cara jumped out of the chair and walked along the terrace.

She didn't have to hear him to know Michael was following. She tried to ignore the fact and stared at the fountain in the garden. The steady stream of water was soothing to her very frazzled nerves.

She felt Michael right behind her. Not touching, but far too close. "When we're married—"

"We're not getting married."

He ignored her interruption and continued, "I can picture how it will be when we're married. I'll just sit with you and we'll talk about our day, share whatever tidbits the other missed. We'll talk about our children."

"Children?" she echoed. "As in the plural of *child?*"

"Seven or eight, at least," he assured her without his usual teasing grin. He looked very serious.

"You've got to be kidding me," she said.

"The number is negotiable," he said, placing a hand on her shoulder. "What were you thinking? More? Ten maybe? You should have a lot of children. You'll be a wonderful mother."

"You have no way of knowing that. I was thinking this one is about all I can handle," she said.

"Three then? It's a nice compromise. Yes, three would be good."

"Three?" she echoed. "Why, we'd be outnumbered."

He gave her hand a quick, comforting squeeze. "One's fine for now. Unless it's twins. I'd like twins. Of course, we'd never dress them the same. I'd want them each to have their own individual identity."

"No way." Cara shook her head. She was desperately afraid one would be her undoing. After all, what did she know about babies?

Nothing.

A big fat *nada*.

It amazed her that Michael seemed so at ease with the idea of a baby…babies.

"Ah, so we agree. If we have twins no rhyming cutesy names, and no dressing them the same. We'll allow them each to pursue their individual interests."

"No twins," she said, praying that it was so.

Twins?

She still hadn't totally wrapped her brain around the idea of being a mother to one.

"Have they done a sonogram yet?" he asked. "Do you know for sure it's not twins?"

"Yes, they did a sonogram right before I left, but no one said anything about twins. And truly, I hope they don't."

She stopped farther along the terrace, staring now at the beautifully manicured garden. Would her baby ever play there?

"Fine." He had followed her and stood close behind her, but not actually touching her. "No twins. But did they tell you the sex yet?"

"It was too early, but even when they can tell, I don't want to know. I prefer being surprised." Even though there was no physical contact, Cara felt as if her every nerve had leaped to attention with Michael's proximity.

What was it about this man?

"A surprise then." He sounded disappointed.

"You'd want to know?" She turned to him. Big mistake. His eyes were so blue. Not a normal blue…brighter somehow. They drew her in, even though she tried not to slip.

"Here's a secret," he said softly, conspiratorially. Small lines crinkled around his eyes. "I peek at my Christmas presents every year. Always have. My mother used to try everything. Hiding them. Duct taping boxes. But I always found them or figured out a way to open them. She couldn't prove I'd seen them, but knew I had. Mothers know those kinds of things. It's just I was never good at surprises. But for you, I'll wait."

Cara smiled at the small glimpse of Michael's past, of his secret present-opening vice.

"If you really want to know, I'm sure Tommy would tell you, but you'd have to promise not to tell me."

He shook his head. "I'll wait with you."

"Thanks." She realized she was holding his hand. It felt right.

"You know," Michael said, "this is the first time we've talked about our baby and you haven't brought up the professor."

"I—" Cara started, ready to assure him that even though she hadn't mentioned Stuart, it didn't mean she wasn't keeping him around. But Michael interrupted.

"Don't—" he warned. "I'm sure you'll have more Professor Stu stories later, but for now let me imagine him dead and buried."

She tsk-tsked. "Poor Stu. It was a tragedy to lose him when he was so young and vibrant."

"Vibrant?" Michael shook his head. "He was a stick-in-the-dirt."

"Mud," Cara corrected him. "The phrase is *stick-in-the-mud*."

"Mud. Dirt. All I know is poor Stu won't be lamented. Won't be missed. It was a tragic, gruesome end. Would you like me to tell you how it happened?"

His grin was infectious and Cara couldn't help but laugh. "You've given this some thought."

"Maybe just a bit," he confessed.

She chuckled.

"I like your laughter. When I walked in on you, Parker and my mother the other day, you were laughing as you discussed flowers. Your laughter, it does something to me. I want to hear it every day. I want to see you smile."

"I—"

"No, don't say anything. You're feeling better now, let's keep it that way."

"My emotions have been somewhat out of control. I've always cried at sappy commercials, but now I don't even have to see them, I just have to think about them and I start tearing up."

"The book said it's hormonal. Normal. Pregnant women have huge mood swings under the best of circumstances. And you've probably got more on your mind than most expectant mothers. Like my marriage proposal."

"You don't give up, do you?"

He pulled her close. "Persistence is my middle name."

"Well, at least it's one of them," she said, teasing him. "You royals sure do load up on the whole name thing."

"That's the way of it. There are just too many relatives we can't afford to offend. Speaking of names," he said, the prince of casualness, "I've been thinking about our baby's name. Do you have any picked out?"

Cara had been thinking about names ever since the pregnancy test had had that little plus sign. "I like more traditional names. Maybe Ruth?"

Michael didn't say a word, he just wrinkled his nose.

"Mary Margaret then?" she tried. "We could call her Maggie."

Another nose wrinkle.

"Okay, Mr. Smarty-pants. What do you suggest?"

"Persephone."

"Ugh." Cara rolled her eyes and made a gagging motion, just in case he didn't understand what *ugh* meant. "Do you want to set this child up for years of abuse from her peers? Persephone?"

"A name should mean something. My many names represent my family history. And *cara mia*—"

"Plain old Cara," she corrected, though that familiar little shiver climbed up her spine as he said it. She'd never admit it to Michael, but his *cara-mias* still affected her.

He just smiled and repeated, "*Cara mia.* It means something to me."

She decided to ignore discussions on just what *cara mia* meant and honed in on the name he wanted to saddle their poor baby with. "But Persephone?"

"Do you know the story?" he asked.

"Mythology, right?"

He nodded. "She was carried away by Hades and her mother, Demeter, was so distraught that she wouldn't allow anything to grow. Finally, Zeus ordered Hades to release Persephone, but it was too late. She'd eaten some seeds and could never truly leave. She was forced to spend a third of her time in the underworld. When she was with her mother, the earth was fertile, a paradise. But when she was with Hades, the land was barren, bereft. Persephone lived a divided life. So will our child, shuttling back and forth between us, never really belonging anywhere."

"Isn't likening us to moving between heaven and hell a bit much?" Cara asked softly, though she knew the truth of Michael's words.

When she left him, she'd be breaking her own heart more than Demeter's ever was.

"No." The sadness in his voice tugged at her.

"*I* will be between heaven and hell—having time with you and then time without. Marry me, *cara mia.*"

"I won't marry someone because I have to."

"I want us to raise our child together. You and me. Marriage is the right thing."

Say the words, she silently begged. *Just tell me you love me and I'll stay.*

With sudden clarity, Cara realized that she needed him to love her because…she loved him.

She might try to deny the feeling. Might rationalize it and tell herself it was too soon to love him. But the truth was, too soon or not, rational or not, she loved him.

Say the words, she silently begged, wanting to tell him her feelings. All he had to do was say there was no have-to involved, only love.

He'd said he desired her, that he'd thought about their night together long after he'd left Erie. But desire wasn't enough. He wanted to be a father to their baby, wanted to build a family. But even that wasn't enough.

He didn't say the words.

And though they were on the tip of Cara's tongue, neither did she.

"I need time to think," she finally whispered.

His hand brushed her now-well-rounded stomach. "There's not much time, sweetheart. And there's so much on the line."

"So much," she sadly echoed.

Her heart.

Her heart was on the line. And all it would take were those three little words to save it from breaking.

"Dinner tonight? Just you and me. The wedding

guests will start arriving soon and then there won't be much time." He paused and added, "No talk of anything serious. Just the two of us, as if we'd just met and I'd asked you out."

"Yes," she said. Maybe if they spent time together he'd figure out that there was more than just a baby between them…. There was love.

Eight

I won't marry someone because I have to.

Cara's words had torn at Michael's heart all day as he got ready for their dinner. He'd given her space, hoping she'd really think about what he said.

I won't marry someone because I have to.

She didn't love him. Didn't have the same feelings for him that he had about her.

Marrying him would be a hardship, would be a necessity. Something she would feel as if she had to do.

All he wanted was what his parents had.

What his sister had found.

All he wanted was a relationship built on love.

Maybe it was too soon for Cara to love him.

I won't marry someone because I have to.

Tonight he'd try to convince her that they had something together, something too big to be ignored.

And he had a good starting point. After all, he knew she desired him. Maybe that could be the basis for something more.

He was going to do his best to see to it that it was.

Michael sliced up olives, trying to concentrate on cooking. Normally he enjoyed being in the kitchen. It felt so everyday, so normal. But today, he couldn't enjoy the process of preparing a meal because his stomach was in knots.

Why did this have to be so hard?

He picked up a tomato and began cutting it into chunks.

He knew that Cara belonged here in Eliason, belonged with him. But she was fighting it, fighting fate.

Someone knocked on his door. He wiped his hand on a towel as he went through the sitting room to open it.

"Hi," Cara said, shyly.

His stomach untwisted slightly at the sight of her. It was as if he could finally breathe again.

She was dressed in a pair of khakis and a solid green polo shirt that was remarkably close to the color of her eyes.

"Hi." He opened the door wide and beckoned her in. "I'm so glad you agreed to dinner."

"I haven't been in this section of the castle before."

"It's my private residence. I do have my own home south of here, but I spend so much time in the capital that I needed something here as well. Living with Mom and Dad is something any self-respecting thirty-year-old should avoid, but there's always a question of security. Having my own wing is my compromise."

"It's lovely."

Michael tried to see the sitting room as she did. Leather furniture, deep red walls, a huge bookcase. It was comfortable, but not nearly as opulent as other areas of the castle.

"I like the books," she added.

He laughed. "That doesn't surprise me."

He guided her to the kitchen. "I'm glad you agreed to dining with me." The words came out much more stilted than he'd have preferred. But he needed to maintain some distance, if only to prevent himself from touching her.

Michael wanted to pull her to him and hold onto her until she agreed to stay. But he'd learned more about Cara. She might be quiet and gentle, but she had a spine of steel.

"Have a seat. I just have a few finishing touches."

"You're cooking?" she asked.

He laughed. "Nervous?"

She shook her head as she slid onto one of the stools on the opposite side of the big island. "No, I imagine if you want to cook, you do it well."

"Why do you say that?"

"Because you're too tenacious to settle for less than that. You'd keep practicing until you got it, right?"

"Tenacious. I think that's a compliment."

"It could be. Or it could be my very polite way of saying that you're a nag."

Michael didn't feel the least bit insulted; in fact, he laughed. "If nagging gets me what I want, then I'm all for it. And what I want—"

She cut him off. "You have a beautiful view." She looked out the windows at the far end of the room.

"See that road?" Michael accepted the fact she wasn't ready to talk about anything heavy. For tonight, he'd try to keep it light. He just wanted to enjoy her company.

Cara looked back at him and he continued. "My great-great-something grandfather was riding on the small dirt predecessor when he spied the hill. He turned to his party and said, *This is where I will build my home.* That's just what he did. Once my family decides to do something, we do. And we've lived in the house he built ever since."

"It's beautiful."

"I know it's not a real castle, the kind with a moat and turret. That's why he built that tall tower, to make up for the lack. He claimed that from the top he could see every corner of Eliason."

"Can you?" Cara asked.

"Eliason is small. In America you've got states that are bigger. But I don't think we're quite that small."

"You have a lot to be proud of. It's so beautiful here. I love going into the city. St. Mark's is so filled with contrasts, history blended with the modern."

"That's what I love as well. My father and I have

been trying to capitalize on just that. Trying to bring in industry, especially computers. We'd like to make Eliason the silicon valley of Europe. At the same time we've tried to capitalize on our history, bringing in tourism...."

Cara listened as Michael talked about his plans for Eliason as he cooked. His excitement was evident. His love for his country infused in every word, in every plan.

When his father stepped down, Michael would lead the country well. And library reading aside, she didn't think she was cut out to help him with a role that large.

Michael served a light salad, followed by a pasta dish with garlic bread and another bottle of sparkling grape juice.

As they ate, he continued to keep the light conversation going.

"Am I boring you?" Michael asked as he glanced her way and their eyes met.

Whenever it happened, Cara felt a connection with him.

"Cara?" he prompted.

"Oh. No, you're not boring me at all. I love your enthusiasm."

Cara could listen to Michael talk forever about anything and feel totally content just to listen. She loved the sound of his voice. Loved the rise and fall of it, loved his cadence.

He led her to a balcony. She'd expected him to pull her into his embrace, but instead he kept a re-

spectful distance. Close, but not too close. She felt
a tiny stab of disappointment.

She looked down at the road his grandfather had
traveled, a road that had led to this castle. More than
a castle, a home.

She inhaled deeply, trying to breathe in the night
air. But all she could smell was Michael. Warm
and…

Inviting.

No matter what she was doing, what was going
on around her, her thoughts just kept circling back
to Michael.

"…and the people insisted…" he continued.

Insisted.

She'd insisted Michael leave her alone. Stop sending her things. Stop asking her to marry him. But he
hadn't obliged and she wasn't sure how to make him.

Of course, he hadn't asked her yet tonight.

She should tell him how she felt. But maybe he'd
confess he didn't feel the same way. That he was at-
tracted to her, liked her, too, but it would never be
anything more. And if he said he simply felt he had
to marry her, she knew her heart would break.

He broke the silence. "We've got so much to talk
about. I've never brought anyone up here. It's my
haven, a place to get away from my duties and the
hectic pace here in the capital."

She couldn't think of anything to say to that, so
she simply said, "Thank you for sharing it."

"Cara, there's so much more I'd like to share with
you if only you'd let me."

She longed to say yes. She might not have known him long, but she was learning more every day about her baby's father.

He was strong.

He was persistent.

Once he set a goal, he didn't back down.

And when he loved, he loved deeply. She had no doubt he loved their baby.

Right now keeping his baby in the country was his goal and to do that he'd do just about anything. Including marrying her.

But this would be a marriage without love. Two people who'd build a life around a child. And what would happen when their comfortable relationship became less than comfortable?

So though she and Michael might be able to build a relationship on their chemistry and the baby—something that might be companionable, even comfortable—in the long run it wouldn't work.

That kind of relationship wasn't what she wanted, what she'd dreamed of. Maybe in time the two of them could grow into something stronger—something built on love.

But time was running out.

Suddenly she knew what she had to do.

"I think I've come up with a solution to our problem," she said, the slight niggle of an idea growing more solid by the second.

"Solution?" he asked. "You're going to say yes and marry me?"

"No. A marriage might work for the short-term,

but when I marry I want it to be because of love, not because of practicalities. Since that's not an option for us…" She paused a fraction of a second, hoping against hope he'd say that love was more than an option, that it was a fact.

When he didn't say the words she longed to hear, she continued, "Since it's not an option, I'm going to move to Eliason. I mean, you need bookstores here. I'll move to St. Mark's. You can see the baby whenever you want."

"That's your solution?"

He didn't sound enthused. As a matter of fact he sounded a great deal less than enthused.

"Yes. It's perfect. Shey will be close, and Parker's going to be coming back and forth between here and Perry Square. I'll still have my friends, and you'll have the baby close by. It's perfect."

"Perfect?" He spat out the word as if it left a bad taste behind.

"Michael, I thought you wanted to be near the baby. This would work without trapping you in a loveless marriage. And you could still see the baby grow up."

"I—" He cut himself off. "I think it's time to say good-night."

He was angry, she could see that, but she wasn't sure why. "But, I want to talk—"

"Not now, Cara. I need some time to digest your offer."

He led her to the door and formally said, "Thank you for dining with me."

"Michael," she started, unsure what to say next.
"Good night."

After Cara left, Michael couldn't stop thinking
about her offer.

He was used to being decisive. But with Cara, he
was feeling uncharacteristically unsure. He was
floundering in the unfamiliar.

He needed advice.

There were only two people he knew he could
count on to give it to him straight. Two people who
needed to be apprised of the situation, not just because they were his parents, but because whatever
happened with Cara would have some impact on the
monarchy.

He knew it was late, but didn't hesitate to head to
their private suite and knock on their door. His father's booming voice called, "Enter."

"Michael." His mother was wearing a pair of
sweatpants and a Brig Niagara T-shirt Parker must
have sent her from Erie. She rose and greeted him
with a hug.

His father was still in his daytime attire and studied him a moment. "It's been years since you came
to us this late. Not since your rather wild teens."

His mother led him to the sofa and sat next to him.
"And we're here, just like we were then. What's
wrong? You haven't been yourself for weeks."

"It's…" Now that he was here, he couldn't think
of the most delicate way to handle his news. "Well,
it's about Cara. And me. You see…"

"I've grown very fond of Cara," his mother assured him. "She's a lovely girl. We'd be delighted to have you see her."

"Well, I have a little more than seeing her in mind. You see, we met before Cara came to Eliason. When I went to visit Parker."

"Go on," his father said.

"It was everything you've told me you experienced when the two of you met. I never imagined falling for anyone the way I fell for her." Knowing he had to say the words, he said, "And she's pregnant with my baby. I know that this will mean a public-relations nightmare…."

His mother waved a hand, stopping him midsentence. "The public can be dealt with at a later date. All I want to know is, how do you feel about Cara? About the baby?"

"I love her, and I'm thrilled at the idea of becoming a father—except when I'm terrified. What if I can't do it? What if I can't be the type of parents you were? Parker and I always knew we came first, despite your very public roles. We were your priority. What if I can't find that balance?"

"You love her, you'll love the baby, and you'll work out the balancing because you know it's important," his father said. "I don't have any doubts about that."

"So when is the wedding?" his mother asked. Then she stopped and smiled. "I'm going to be a grandmother. Oh." Tears welled in her eyes. "I'll warn you right now, Michael, that this baby is going to be spoiled. I have plans. And so many presents to buy."

Michael could see the wheels in her mind turning as she considered all the ways she could spoil this baby.

"Your plans?" his father simply asked.

"I've asked her to marry me…repeatedly. She won't. She says she doesn't want to be forced into marriage." Just saying the words sent another sharp stab of pain radiating through his body. "Although, tonight she offered to relocate to Eliason, so that I could be near my child."

"Ah, the Dillonetti curse." His father shook his head. "The men in our family never choose an easy path to love. We have to work at it. Convincing your mother to accept my proposal…"

"Don't listen to him. I said yes the first time he asked."

"More like the twentieth. I counted."

"The first nineteen weren't serious proposals. Number twenty, that was the first one you really meant. You'd thought it all through and decided your country could handle an American as their future queen."

"So, you think there's a chance Cara will say yes?"

His mother kissed his cheek. "She'd be a fool not to."

Michael knew he should have come to his parents sooner. Having them behind him meant everything. He hadn't realized how much he needed their reassurance.

"Wait a minute," his mother said. She rose and

went into the bedroom, returning a minute later with
a small box. "Your grandfather gave me this. It was
your grandmother's engagement ring. If you want it,
I'd like you to have it for your Cara."

Michael opened the box and found an exquisite
diamond surrounded by topazes. "It's beautiful."

His father's expression said it all—his look telling her how much he appreciated her gesture.

He turned to Michael. "Don't rush her. Our family
falls fast and hard. But maybe she needs to fall slower
and softer. You may have to ask twenty times, and that
might feel like an eternity, but if you love her—"

"I do," he assured his father.

"Then it's worth the wait."

"Give her some breathing room," his mother
added. "Finding out she's pregnant, that's a lot to
deal with in and of itself. Love her. Support her. Wait
for her to take whatever time she needs. Woo her
gently. Convince her that it's her you want. That you
want Cara and not just the mother of your baby."

"Of course it's Cara I want."

"Remind her of that, but go slow."

"Give her space?" Michael muttered.

"That's just it." His mother smiled. "Now, when
exactly is my first grandchild due? I have so many
things to get ready."

Michael filled his mother and father in on everything, even as he wondered how he was going to give
Cara breathing room, when every fiber of his being
wanted her more with each passing moment.

Nine

Cara knew Michael was avoiding her.

It didn't take a rocket scientist to figure it out. He wasn't exactly being subtle.

Wherever she was, Michael wasn't. And if their paths accidentally did cross, he uncrossed them as quickly as possible.

He wasn't rude. Just distant.

There were no more flowers. No more marriage proposals.

Instead of lurking through the back corridors, she was striding down the busiest passageways, hoping for something.

If pressed, he'd give her a small social smile, or ask about her health. But that was the extent of their communication.

It was driving Cara crazy.

She missed him. She didn't miss the gifts, she just missed him. Missed that crooked grin every time he felt he was getting away with something.

Missed those little bows that had driven her nuts.

She missed the feel of him when he held her.

She missed his hand lightly brushing her stomach.

She missed his teasing.

She missed his kisses.

She felt as if she were walking around with a hole somewhere. Something was missing.

Not something. Someone. Michael.

When she'd blurted out that she'd decided to stay in Eliason, it had been a rash, spur of the moment decision. Sort of like the night she'd met Michael.

Note to self…no more acting on her gut feelings.

Logic.

Well-thought-out plans.

That's how she was going to run her life from now on.

She was going to go back to weighing everything before she acted.

"Cara?" Shey called. She had arrived last night and they were spending the day catching her up on the wedding plans.

"He's looking at you again," Parker told her.

Cara turned and glanced across the room where Michael stood with Tanner and Jace. Her eyes met his. Rather than that slow, sexy smile, he looked pained.

She sighed.

"What on earth is going on now? Problems?" Parker asked.

"Nope," Cara answered, deciding to pretend she thought Parker was asking about the wedding, even though she knew her friend was asking about Michael. "No problems. The wedding's getting close, but we've got everything under control. Just look at this, Shey…."

She flipped to the seating chart that had taken her days to get just right.

"You definitely have a problem," Shey said.

"No way. I went over this chart a dozen times. No feuding relatives are seated at the same table, no—"

Shey waved the chart aside, obviously not the least bit concerned about who sat where. "Parker said you have to talk to me later."

Shey was glowing with happiness. There hadn't been a chance to really talk yet, but Cara knew that it was only a matter of time.

"Later, I promise." Much later if she had her way.

"I hate being out of the loop," Shey muttered.

"I'll reloop you after your guests have arrived and been settled," Cara promised.

The first wave of Perry Square guests were due to arrive any minute. Maybe they'd provide enough of a distraction to buy Cara some time.

Time to figure out what was up with Michael.

As if on cue, a man Cara hadn't met walked into the room and addressed Michael. "Your guests have arrived, Your Highness."

"I do want answers soon," Shey said as they followed the crowd to the front hall.

Despite her worries, Cara couldn't help but feel a wave of anticipation. Pearly was due to be in this first group.

She checked and spotted the ambassador standing next to Michael across the hall.

"I'm so excited," Parker said for the umpteenth time. "What do you think they'll do when they see each other?"

Cara was about to answer that she didn't know, but she didn't have a chance to get the words out because the door opened and a huge group of their friends walked in.

Cries of welcome filled the huge foyer.

Libby, Josh and their children, Meg and J.T. Joe, Louisa and their children, Aaron and Ella. Mac and Mia and their daughters, Katie and Merry. Then came Sarah and Donovan, who were expecting their first child at Christmas.

Cara felt a pull of kinship with Sarah.

She'd love to talk babies with her, but it would have to wait until after the wedding. She'd tell everyone then. With the way her stomach was expanding lately, they'd all guess if she didn't tell them soon.

Jace ran up to hug his sister Shelly and her twins, Amanda and Bobby, as they entered. Cara noted that Tanner's bodyguard, Peter, was close at hand. When Jace let Shelly go, Peter slipped his arm over her shoulder. It was obvious that things between them were going well. Cara was happy for them.

Mabel and her boyfriend Elmer walked in with Josie and her beau Hoffman.

Last but not least, Pearly Gates came in carrying a huge purple bag.

Cara held her breath as she held hands with Shey and Parker, and the three of them edged closer to the ambassador.

Pearly was almost next to him before he spied her.

"Pearly?" the ambassador whispered. "Pearly Gates?" he said louder this time.

Pearly turned. Cara knew the moment realization struck. Their friend's face paled as she studied her old boyfriend a moment. Her initial reaction was to smile, but that abruptly faded.

"You!" was all she said.

Not a joyous, I've-found-you-after-all-these-years sort of *you*, but a *you* that came out more like a swearword.

"Pearly." The ambassador's astonishment was evident. "You're here in Eliason."

He leaned forward, as if he were going to hug her.

Pearly pushed him back. "Buster McClinnon, you mangy, worm-eatin', lily-livered cad."

Cara's heart sank as she realized her fantasy reunion—wasn't.

"Pearly?" the ambassador asked, clearly confused.

"Don't you Pearly me. I—" She stuttered and sputtered and finally said, "Don't you come near me, you sweet-talkin' womanizer."

Pearly abruptly walked out of the room.

Cara glanced at Parker, who'd been cornered by some of their Perry Square guests. And Shey, never one for overly emotional scenes, backed up, leaving Cara to deal with the ambassador.

"Sir?" she asked, expecting him to be devastated his old girlfriend wasn't happy to meet him again.

"She hasn't changed a bit," he said, smiling. "Not one bit."

He sounded almost proud.

"I owe you an apology. When you started reminiscing about the girl you lost, I recognized her. I mean, how many Pearly Gates could one country hold?"

"One planet," he corrected with a chuckle.

Cara felt a wave of relief. He wasn't hurt. She smiled. "I see your point. More than one Pearly? It boggles the imagination. I wanted to surprise you. I thought reuniting you both would be sweet. I didn't mean—"

She didn't get a chance to explain what she didn't mean. The ambassador had swept her up in his arms and was squeezing her in a warm embrace.

"Pearly Gates. You brought me my Pearly." He set her down. "Tell me everything. How you know her, what she's been doing all these years. Everything."

Cara began to tell him about Pearly and her place on the square. Slowly, some of the others joined in, and after introductions were made, they began to share as well.

Pearly *was* the Square and the stories of her help, and her meddling, were legendary.

"Does Pearly really have a cousin Lerlene?" Libby Gardner asked.

At that point the ambassador joined in with stories of his own.

Slowly, Cara eased away from the crowd. It didn't take long for her to find Pearly.

Pearly caught sight of Cara and looked as if she were going to make a break for it.

"Wait," Cara called. "Please."

The older woman stopped. Pearly, who always had a huge smile that was only surpassed by her even bigger heart, had tears in her eyes.

"You knew, didn't you? How could you?" she asked.

"We thought you'd be pleased. I never thought seeing the ambassador, Buster, again would hurt you. I wanted to surprise you," she tried to explain.

"You did," Pearly assured her, a hitch in her voice.

"We hoped it would be a pleasant one," Cara corrected.

Pearly sighed and dabbed at her eyes with a tissue. "Maybe it was. I just made a fool of myself, didn't I?"

"No," Cara assured her. "You were just caught off guard."

"Yeah, I was that."

"You've talked about the ambassador in the past, and we all thought…" She let the sentence trail off not knowing what else to say about their obviously misguided plans.

Pearly took her hand. "You all were right. I'm just a foolish old woman."

"Pearly, you're anything but foolish and you'll never be old. You're wise and…" She searched for an appropriate term, "Experienced."

Pearly laughed. "I guess that's a nice way to put it."

"Do you want to talk about what happened to you and the ambassador?" Cara asked gently. "I'll under-stand if you don't."

Pearly sat on a sofa and Cara sat next to her.

"It was so silly. He'd graduated from college and come home for the summer. It was August when he invited me out for dinner. Not just the local burger place, which was our normal haunt. No, he asked me to McIlhiney's, a ten-star dining sort of place. It was going to be a special night he told me and I thought, I mean we'd always talked about…"

"You thought he was going to ask you to marry him?" Cara asked.

"Yes." Pearly sighed wistfully. "But he didn't. He told me he was going to school for his master's de-gree and expected me to toast his leaving me behind. Again. I just couldn't. I was so mad and I'll confess, I egged on a fight. Then it was the end of summer and we were still fighting when he left. I saw him about a year later. He brought a girl. And…well, here we are. He's an ambassador and I'm just a beau-tician."

"There's no *just* about you, Pearly. You are a spe-cial lady. Don't you know how much you mean to all of us? I don't think there's anyone you haven't helped at one time or another."

"What you're saying is, I'm a busybody?" she asked with a watery smile.

"What I'm saying is we all love you and really thought that seeing the ambassador again would make you happy."

Cara reached out and hugged Pearly. "Like I said, maybe it did. It's just I was taken by surprise. Like the time Stella from the five-and-dime was wearing a skirt with a pair of those thong panties under it. When the wind caught her skirt and blew it up, all she had was that glorified thread up her backside.... Well, it was that kind of surprise both for her and everyone else in the vicinity."

"You feel like you have a thread up your back-side?" Cara asked, trying not to smile.

Pearly laughed. "Yes, something like that." .

She seemed to pull herself together. "Let's go back to the others. I'm not the type of person who runs away from a difficult situation."

They started walking back toward the guests. Pearly turned to Cara and said, "Don't think I haven't noticed there's something different about you."

"Pardon?" Oh, darn. Cara looked down and didn't think she looked that much more pregnant, not enough that anyone would notice. But Pearly was studying her.

"Yes, something's different about you, though I can't put my finger on it. And something's bother-ing you." Pearly patted her shoulder. "Look at me, comin' in here caterwaulin' about the nice surprise you planned and not even noticin' you've got prob-lems. Do you want to talk about it now?"

"If I said no would you let it drop?" Cara asked, not holding out much hope.

"That's not very likely. But it might buy you some time. Normally I'd start pestering you right now, but I need a bit to get my feet back under me."

Cara blew out a breath of relief.

"But," Pearly said slowly, "I would imagine this evening I'd be feeling up to a conversation."

"And a story?"

"Always." She pulled back her shoulders and stood up straight. "Now, let's go see ol' Buster. I'm a wonderin' just what he's been up to all these years."

"So what was between the ambassador and your friend?"

Michael met up with Cara after dinner. He'd watched her throughout the meal and was concerned. She looked out of sorts, and he wondered if he should call the doctor.

Before she could answer, he asked, "Are you all right?"

"I'm fine. As for what was up earlier with Pearly, well, it was simply a surprise for her to find the ambassador here. Not that he was an ambassador back when she knew him. He was just Buster then."

"And her reaction when she's surprised is to turn around and run out of a room crying?"

Cara just shrugged.

"Women. The species baffles me. The ambassador was surprised as well, but he didn't burst into tears."

"Yes, we all know that men are good at not disclosing their feelings. And jeez, it's so manly and all. We women just love that quality about the gender."

Sarcasm.

Every now and then his sweet Cara added that bite to whatever she was saying. Sometimes Michael admired the trait.

Right now was not one of those times.

He'd spent the last few days driving himself crazy, trying to give Cara space like his parents had suggested.

But giving space didn't seem to be endearing him to her. As a matter of fact, she looked downright annoyed with him. Annoyed and sarcastic. That was not the goal.

"I think we need to talk," he told her. "Alone."

"Oh, we're talking again?" There it was again— that bite in her tone. "After the other day when you stopped talking to me because you were pouting about not getting your way, well, I thought—"

"I do not pout," he felt obliged to point out.

"Oh, you do pout like some little boy who didn't get his way. You tell me you want to marry me and when I say no, I won't ever marry because I have to, you run off and pout."

"I—"

She interrupted him. She was on a roll now and couldn't seem to stop. "And rather than acting pleased when I agree to throw my whole life into disarray, leave my home, my friends and my business in order to come here just so you can be close to your baby, you stop talking to me."

"Later. When everyone's settled, we'll talk. I've given you space, given you time, but that's done now. It's time we settled some things once and for all."

"Oh, the prince decreed it and this mere serf had better obey or else—"

Michael knew he was the soul of patience, but even a patient man could only be pushed so far. He silenced her in the most effective way he knew.

He kissed her.

He pulled her into his arms and held her, he didn't just explore her lips with his own, he feasted. No gentle introduction, but raw and fevered need.

How could she not see how much he needed her? He understood and appreciated her offer to move to St. Mark's, to come to Eliason so he could be near their child, but that wasn't enough.

How could she not understand that nothing but marriage, a lifetime together, would suffice. They were meant to be together. He used the kiss to try and show her. He wanted her to remember just how good they could be.

She made a small noise in the back of her throat and twined her arms around his neck.

He pulled back and whispered, "This is what we could have, *cara mia*. Just say yes."

"I—"

"Well, well, well," a woman's voice said from behind Michael.

Cara twisted out of his embrace, her face flaming red. "Shey, I was going to come find you when I was done here."

"The way that kiss looked, I'd've been waiting a long, long time," she said with a grin.

She walked up to Michael and thrust out her hand. "We've had our nice social introduction, but since you're up tight and personal with my friend here, I suppose something more is required. I'm Shey, your sister and Cara's partner in the stores. And it seems to me I've heard your sister talk about your many dalliances…."

She turned to Cara and said, "I've been practicing more appropriate language now that I'm about to be a princess. It's a strain, I can tell you."

Cara assured her, "Dalliance was good."

"Thanks." Now to Michael, she continued, "Since I've heard the stories, I feel compelled to warn you that if you hurt Cara, I'll be coming after you."

"Shey," Cara said, "the come-after-you part wasn't overly princess-y."

"Yeah, I know. I can only maintain the princess thing for so long, then the Harley rider in me kicks into gear."

"I'm a big girl." Cara stepped next to Michael.

He was surprised to feel her hand slip into his.

"I know that," Shey started to say.

Cara shook her head. "No, I don't think you do. You and Parker are the best friends anyone could want and you've both taught me so much. I may be quiet, I may be a lot more easygoing than you two—"

Michael couldn't help it, he made a scoffing sound. "I hope you were going to add that you've learned to be more stubborn and difficult than my sister ever managed, and that's saying something."

"Cara difficult?" Shey asked, sounding surprised.

Despite the fact the woman had threatened him, Michael liked her. He smiled and assured her, "Sarcastic and stubborn."

"Way to go." Shey beamed like a proud mother who'd just learned her child had won an award.

"And thank you for the warning, Shey," Michael said. "But maybe it's Cara you need to warn against dallying with *my* heart."

Shey looked puzzled.

"I asked her to marry me. Surely she's told you that?"

"No, I don't believe that's been mentioned yet."

Shey was no longer glaring at him. No, she'd turned her ire on Cara.

"Actually, I've asked her repeatedly. She keeps turning me down. I'm a dalliance for *her.* She's breaking my heart."

Cara made a small growl, which made Michael grin. "Well, it looks like I should allow you two ladies to catch up. Cara, I'll see you later and we'll have that talk."

He made a very courtly bow, then walked down the hall whistling.

Michael walked out of the room and Cara couldn't help enjoying the view as he left, even though part of her wanted nothing more than to kick that particular asset.

He was such a spoiled, pouty tattletale.

Shey cleared her throat. "Earth calling Cara. If you can tear your eyes off your Prince Charming, maybe I can get some answers. For instance, what was that all about? And I really want to know about the difficult thing."

"I'm not being difficult, despite what Michael says. He's just pouting because I won't marry him."

"He mentioned that. He's asked more than once and you keep telling him no?"

"Yes. Are you sure you want to hear all this now? Wouldn't you rather go down and see the wedding cake, or how about some floral designs?"

"Cake, shmake. And flowers have never interested me. What I want to know is why a man you've only known a few weeks has asked you more than once to marry him? And why, seeing the interest in your eyes as you watched him leave, you've said no?"

"About the few weeks thing. It's not quite accurate. You see, I met Michael before I came to Eliason. He came to Erie to try and talk Parker into coming home and I bumped into him."

Shey's eyes narrowed and she studied Cara. "And? You bumped into him and…?"

"I'm pregnant."

"That was some bumping," Shey said as she sank onto a chair. "I think I need to let you give me the whole story."

"There's not much to tell. We bumped, there was a misunderstanding and we both went on with our lives, never even knowing each other's real name. I found out I was expecting, and planned to tell you and Parker after the wedding, but then I came here, met Michael, discovered my baby's father is a prince and passed out."

"Passed out. Parker mentioned that," Shey said.

"I was fine. Tommy said—"

"Wait, who's Tommy? Maybe I'm getting old, or maybe this wedding stuff has addled my brain, but I can't keep up."

Cara sighed. She'd wanted to get the explanation over as quickly as possible, but backtracked. "Tommy's a doctor. And then Michael figured out I was pregnant, asked me to marry him and of course I said no."

"Of course?" she echoed.

"Of course. There are so many reasons why I can't say yes. Mainly he just asked because he's an honorable man who wants to be with his baby. So, I plan to tell everyone Professor Stuart is the father."

"You've got another man?" Shey raked her hand through her short red hair. "And we always thought you were the shy one. Let me get this straight, not only are you expecting the prince's baby, you've got another man on the side I didn't know about."

"No, there is no Professor Stu. I made him up. But Michael can't really have an illegitimate child, so the professor will be the father, and Michael can be the baby's godfather or something. My connection with Parker will make that seem reasonable. And," she said, reaching the part that she hadn't discussed with

Parker yet, "I will be making plans to move to Elia-son so Michael can be with the baby as often as he likes."

"You're leaving the Square?"

"Look at it this way," Cara said, "Amar is practically around the corner, so you and I will see each other. And Parker will be coming to Eliason, so I'll see her, too."

"But you're moving to a new country and having a baby on your own?"

"I can't take the baby away from Michael. He has responsibilities here and can't come to Perry Square, so I have to come here. Maybe we can open a second Titles and Monarch's here. We'll be an international chain." Cara was babbling, but she couldn't stand the way Shey was staring at her. She felt like she was under a microscope.

Shey ignored talk of international chains and zeroed in on the real issue. "You love him."

Cara couldn't lie to her friend. "Yes. But he doesn't love me. He's a good man. A noble man. But he doesn't love me."

Shey shook her head and looked disgusted. "That's crap."

"Pardon?"

"Come with me." Shey grabbed her hand and pulled her out the door.

"Where are we going?"

"To find Parker. The three of us have to talk. We'll figure something out."

Cara pulled her hand from Shey's and stopped

cold. "*We* won't figure anything out. I've already decided what I'm going to do."

"But—"

"Don't interrupt. I love you both, but I have to do this my way. Yes, I love Michael, but I won't ever marry him when all he feels for me is obligation and a healthy dose of lust. When I marry it will be to someone who loves me as much as I love him. That's not going to happen with Michael, so the best I can do is make plans that will be as fair to both of us as possible. I've made up my mind. There's nothing for the three of us to figure out."

She turned to leave. A grand exit.

"Michael's right, you sure did learn to be stubborn," Shey called. There was more than a hint of pride in her voice.

Cara turned and smiled at her, then left. She needed some time to pull herself together before Michael caught up with her again.

She was going to have to be as firm with him as she'd been with Shey.

She wasn't going to marry a man out of obligation.

When and if she ever married, it would be for one reason only…because they *both* loved each other.

Ten

It was a comedy of errors. Every time Cara finally caught up with Michael, something or someone interrupted.

The queen would appear with a matter that needed her attention right away.

The king would drag Michael off to a meeting.

One of the growing number of guests would join them, not realizing they were interrupting.

At this rate Cara figured they'd be celebrating the baby's first birthday before they had time alone.

Michael's home might be huge, but it felt crowded.

And here it was, the day before the wedding, and Cara knew they wouldn't solve anything soon. She had a list of things to do a mile long, and she was sure his mother had given him one of the same length.

The queen had turned into a bit of a wedding tyrant.

Cara was trying to decide what needed to be done first, when she practically ran into him.

"Michael," she said, drinking in the sight of him.

"Hurry, before someone spots us. In here." Michael pulled her into a small office Cara had never seen before.

"Is this yours?" she asked.

"Yes." He took her folder and set it on a table, then lightly brushed his hand over her stomach.

"How are you?"

"I'm fine. It's been crazy." She studied the room. "I pictured your office as something more ornate. Gilt, antiques. This is…"

She looked for a word to describe the room. The desk was old, but not an antique sort of old, but rather a someone-was-about-to-leave-it-out-for-the-rubbish way. There were plain but functional shelves on all four walls. They were crammed with books and papers. Files even.

She'd been to his private quarters and knew they were neat and tidy. She'd have expected his office to be much the same, but this…this was chaos.

"Do the cleaning people know where this room is?" she asked.

"Yes, and they know it's off-limits. This is my personal space. You may have noticed that privacy is a luxury here. And I like it as is. It's close to the center of things, but private. That makes it the perfect place for us to talk."

"There's—" Cara was going to finish the sentence with *nothing to talk about,* but she couldn't because Michael had pulled her into his arms and kissed her. And rather than break off the kiss, she welcomed it. She'd missed being in his embrace.

When he finally released her, she said, "You're trying to kiss me into a stupor, hoping I'll be so muddled I won't be able to argue with you."

"I have no doubts that no matter how muddled you are, you'll find a way to argue. When I first met you there was a blaze of awareness, desire. But now that I've gotten to know you better, there's more. You're an aggravating, stubborn woman and I've been waiting for you…."

His voice trailed off and they realized they weren't the only ones in the area. There were voices in the hall. The door burst open and Pearly Gates barreled into the room, the ambassador on her heels.

The ambassador looked embarrassed. "I'm so sorry. We thought the room was empty."

"Cara, tell this lily-livered cad to stop followin' me," Pearly said.

"Cara, tell this stubborn, won't-listen-to-reason, old woman that I—"

Cara didn't have time to tell either one of them anything. Pearly turned on the ambassador. "Old? I happen to know which one of us is older, Buster boy."

"Which is why we don't have time to waste," the ambassador said. "We've waited too long as it is."

"Waiting?" Pearly asked. "I know all about waiting. I'm good at it. After all, I waited for years for him to say the words, and he never did."

"What words?" the ambassador asked, looking confused. "All through school all I could think of was coming home to you, of building a life with you."

"And all it would have taken were those words. I loved you so much, and you didn't love me at all. You were used to me. I couldn't go into a lopsided relationship. Loving you, knowing you desired me, even liked me, but didn't love me… It would have killed my love eventually."

"Didn't love you?" He closed the space between them and took Pearly into his arms. "Didn't love you? I worshipped the ground you walked on. No one then, or since, has ever stood up to me the way you did, do. No one's ever made me feel half the things you have. Didn't love you? Pearly Gates, you're a fool. I loved you so much. All these years I've loved you. I've never met any woman who could make me feel half of what you did…do."

"Too late," Pearly whispered. "It's too late."

"Not too late, you fool. Say yes now. As soon as we see these children married, I'll whisk you off and make an honest woman of you."

"But—"

"Make an honest man of me, Pearly. We've both grown over the years. There are so many new things we have to discover about each other. But under all that we're still Pearly and Buster, still meant for each other. I still love you."

Pearly Gates, a woman known on Perry Square for always having something to say, stood speechless.

"Pearly?" the ambassador prompted.

"Yes," she said, her voice firm.

"Is that a yes, what-do-you-want? Or is it a yes-I'll-marry-you-and-make-you-the-happiest-man-on-earth?" he asked.

"The last one, the I'll-marry-you one. I love you, you old fool."

The older gentleman pulled Pearly into his arms and kissed her right and proper.

"I think we're embarrassing the children." Pearly looked at them as if she suddenly remembered she wasn't alone in the room with Buster. "Cara, honey, thanks for helping us sort that all out."

"I didn't do anything," Cara assured her.

Pearly walked over and hugged her. "You've done more than you know. And let me do you a favor. Don't make the same mistake I did. Don't let pride stand in the way of your happiness. Tell the boy what you need from him, don't leave him guessing."

She walked back to the ambassador and took his hand. "Come on, Buster. I think we interrupted a long overdue conversation."

She led him out of the room and closed the door firmly.

"Well," Michael said. "That was interesting."

Cara sniffed. "That was beautiful. Just beautiful."

"What about Pearly's advice? Are you going to leave me guessing? Tomorrow's the wedding. I want to be there with your friends. The two of us in front with them. Just say the words. Say you'll marry me."

"This is getting old. I can't."

"You won't, despite the fact you want to. And it's not just the fact I'm a prince that's scaring you off. It's not just that you don't want to *have* to get married. It's more and you know it. It would have been more honest if you'd told me up front you don't care about me the way I care for you."

"Care? You think I don't care? If you only knew the half of it."

"Then why? Tell me what you need from me," he implored, his voice ragged.

"It's the—" She searched for a reason, one that didn't involve her begging him to love her. "It's the whole prince thing."

"Parker's marrying a private investigator, and your friend Shey is marrying a prince. Why can't we be together?"

"Don't you see I'm nothing special? Parker is a princess, but she's also a very practical woman who is strong enough to buck expectations and go after the life—the man—she wants. Shey's the same way. Strong. She has causes, ideas she'll fight for. She'll be a wonderful princess, despite not being born into the position. But me? I'm just Cara. Shy. Quiet. A bookworm. I'm more at home reading about life than living it. What would I have to offer your country?"

"Cara, what would you have told our baby if you hadn't found me?" he asked, ignoring her comments entirely. "Would you have kept the professor alive?"

That's it? No arguments. No list of reasons why she could be a princess? Just asking what she'd tell their baby about its father.

"I would have told him or her—will tell him or her—that I met their daddy on a magical night. That we had so much in those few hours it was enough to last me a lifetime. Because like all magic, it faded the next day. But there was a little magic left behind. Our baby."

"Magic. That about sums it up for me. But you're wrong, sometimes the magic doesn't fade. Sometimes it lasts." He took her hand. "I think you could be happy here, with me. But if you can't, if you really can't, then I'll stand by and let you go. Professor Stu can be resurrected. I'll let you both go."

"You'd do that? Just let me walk away with the baby, when I know how much you already love it?"

"I'd do that and so much more for you because I love you. I want what's best for you and our baby. I'd like to think that's me, but if it's not…" He let the sentence hang a moment, then added, "You've seen what a life here would be. Being a part of the royal family has its perks, but it also has its burdens. I can't walk away from it."

"Say it again," she murmured, not sure she'd heard him right.

"Magic—"

"No, the other part."

"Love. You have my heart. My love. Surely you knew that."

"Surely I didn't." Tears welled up in her eyes.

There was no blaming pregnancy this time. Her heart was overflowing and there was no place for all those emotions to go except out.

"Of course, I love you. I wouldn't have asked you to marry me if I didn't."

"For the baby. You said you wanted to raise the baby here and I figured I was just part of the package."

"*Cara mia,* that night… It sounds trite, impossible even, but that night I fell in love with you. You showed me a glimpse of what my parents have had all these years. I never believed in love at first sight, until the moment I looked in your eyes and knew in the center of my soul that you were who I'd been waiting for all these years. And the more I've been with you, the more I've known you, the more that feeling has grown. I would have asked you to marry me if you weren't expecting our baby because I can't imagine a life without you."

"I—"

"Say yes. I know it's fast, I know it's scary, but trust in what we have and say yes."

"I was going to say I love you. Then I was going to add, yes."

He reached in his pocket and pulled out a ring. Not just any ring. A huge diamond surrounded by topazes. "This was my father's mother's ring. My mother gave it to me when I told them about marrying you."

"And the baby?"

"Yes, they know. They haven't said anything at my request, but they're bursting at the seams."

He slid the ring on her finger. "If you don't like it, we can get another."

Cara just studied it. "It's beautiful."

"I've had it in my pocket every day. Just waiting for you."

"All I was waiting for was the words. I do love you," she assured him, wrapping her arms around him.

"Do you think you can get ready to get married tomorrow?" he asked.

She laughed. "It seems I have connections in Eliason. I'm pretty sure I can swing it."

Cara stood in the front of the chapel, surrounded by friends and family. Her heart was full as she glanced at the man by her side.

"Do you Cara Marie Phillips take this man, Antonio Michael Paul Mickovich Dillonetti…"

She looked at Michael, her baby's father, the man she loved, and said, "I do."

The question was repeated. "Do you Marie Anna Parker Mickovich Dillonetti…"

And one last time, "Do you Shey Ann Carlson…"

Each of her friends echoed her, "I do."

Cara glanced over her shoulder and saw her mother and father sitting in the front pew with the rest of the parents. Michael had flown them in as a surprise. Right behind them, Pearly was sitting next to the ambassador.

Cara knew that sometimes something was just too strong not to be, no matter how long it took.

Call it magic.

Call it fate.

Call it destiny.

Call it love.

Her eyes met Michael's and he mouthed the words *I love you.*

Cara knew just what she planned to call it….

"I now pronounce you husband and wife…." The minister paused, and chuckled, as he added, "And husband and wife, and husband and wife."

Cara looked at her friends and their husbands, then stepped into her husband's open arms.

Yes, she knew just what she was going to call it….

Happily ever after.

Epilogue

"**P**rince Paul Michael Stuart Ericson Mickovich Dillonetti." Cara cradled the hour old dark haired baby who seemed far too small for such a grand name.

"Cara," Michael said. She could tell he was trying to be stern, but neither of them had stopped smiling since the baby was born.

To be honest, she wasn't sure she'd stopped smiling since the wedding. She couldn't believe how happy the last few months had been. And now, holding their baby, her happiness level seemed to be expanding exponentially.

"Oh, come on, Michael. It's a great name. Nice and long like you royals seem to require. There's one name for your father, one for you—"

"But Stuart?"

"Of course, Stuart. After all, he was instrumental in getting us together." She laughed simply because her joy needed somewhere to go. she felt giddy with it.

Michael reached out and gently stroked her cheek. "Stuart it is, then. After what you went through bringing him into the world, you could call him Bubba for all I care."

"Honey, I meant it as a joke." Michael had seemed to suffer more than she had through the delivery. Holding the baby, the memory of the pain had all but faded.

"*Cara mia,* there was nothing remotely funny about labor. You'll never go through it again."

She handed the baby to him, noting he—the father—did look rather pale.

"He's perfect, Michael. I don't want to have him be an only child."

"Cara—"

"Fine. We'll wait at least a year before we start on a sibling."

She waited for him to protest, but realized he was engrossed in studying their son.

"He is perfect."

She put a hand on Michael's shoulder, the other on the baby's chest. She was totally content. She'd already talked to Parker and Shey. They were both coming to Eliason next week to visit and meet the baby.

This last year had been an amazing change. At

first, it had seemed scary, but now, she couldn't imagine Parker without Jace, or Shey without Tanner. And in her wildest dreams, she couldn't imagine her life without the man who was currently cradling their son.

When she said I do to Michael, she thought she'd found her happily-ever-after. But now, watching her husband cradling their son, she knew the wedding was just the start of a lifetime of happily-ever-afters.

Her heart was overflowing.

"Now, about the baby's sister…" she started again. Laughter filled the room.

A lifetime of happily-ever-after—that's what she'd discovered.

* * * * *

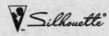

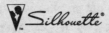

SILHOUETTE *Romance*®

COMING NEXT MONTH

#1786 MUCH ADO ABOUT MATCHMAKING—
Myrna Mackenzie
Shakespeare in Love
Can the stage for love really be set by a well-intentioned
matchmaker's trickery, a villainous relative and a gorgeous hotel?
Independent, career-minded Emmaline Carstairs wants little to do
with ex-military businessman Ryan Benedict. Still, the roles her
uncle coerces them into playing seem more natural every moment…
and a wedding might just be the final act!

#1787 THE TEXAN'S SUITE ROMANCE—
Judy Christenberry
Lone Star Brides
Filling in as a publicist, Tabitha Tyler finds herself butting heads
with writer Alex Myerson as they embark on a book tour. But as
traveling difficulties bring them closer, Tabitha begins to see another
side to Alex. And it's not long before she embarks on her most
difficult campaign to date—convincing the widowed author
to start a new chapter in his life with her.

#1788 LIGHTS, ACTION…FAMILY!—Patricia Thayer
Love at the Goodtime Café
Hired to be a stuntman for a movie being shot on her family ranch,
Reece McKellen instantly attracts Emily Hunter's eye. And it's
not long before their off-screen chemistry has Emily wondering if
the handsome stranger and his niece might not provide the most
important scene in her life.…

#1789 HER GYPSY PRINCE—Crystal Green
Blossom County Fair
The Gypsy Prince captivated Elizabeth Dupres immediately, even as
she picketed his carnival. Although they came from vastly different
worlds, she is powerless to deny her attraction to him. And now
Elizabeth must decide if she will let this wandering man walk out of
her life forever or stand up to her family to embrace his love.

SRCNM0905